ANOOKA'S ANSWER

ANOOKA'S ANSWER

by **Marjorie Cowley**
Illustrated by **Bryn Barnard**

Clarion Books • New York

Clarion Books
a Houghton Mifflin Company imprint
215 Park Avenue South, New York, NY 10003
Text copyright © 1998 by Marjorie Cowley
Illustrations copyright © 1998 by Bryn Barnard

Text is 12/15 point New Century Schoolbook.

Printed in the U.S.A.

Library of Congress Cataloging-in-Publication Data
Cowley, Marjorie.
Anooka's answer / by Marjorie Cowley ; illustrated by Bryn Barnard.
p.   cm.
Companion to: Dar and the spear-thrower.
Summary: While living in a river valley in southern France during the
Upper Paleolithic era, thirteen-year-old Anooka rejects the ways of her
clan and sets out to make another kind of life for herself.
ISBN 0-395-88530-2
1. Magdalenian culture—France—Juvenile fiction. [Magdalenian cul-
ture—France—Fiction. 2. Prehistoric peoples—Fiction. 3. Sex roles—
Fiction.] I. Barnard, Bryn, ill. II. Title.
PZ7.C8377An   1998
[Fic]—dc21   98-4800
CIP
AC

VB   10   9   8   7   6   5   4   3   2   1

My gratitude to all those who gave me precious
gifts of honest comment and steadfast support
during the slow blossoming of this book
—M.C.

For my daughter, Wynn
—B.B.

CONTENTS

1. The Lion Cub Waits   1
2. Singing on the Riverbank   11
3. Bears   19
4. The Dance of the Salmon Spirit   24
5. Chee-boy   30
6. Sisters   39
7. The Secret Cave   44
8. Intruder   52
9. The *Toc* Call   56
10. Telling Nomi   65
11. The Singing Bow   70
12. The Vigil   76
13. Transformations   80
14. Preparations   90
15. Night Creature   95
16. Circle of Fire   102
17. Tracking   108
18. Coming Closer   114
19. The Fork in the River   122
20. Anooka's Answer   133
21. Awakening   140
    Author's Note   148

The story of a young girl nearing adulthood, who lived 12,000 years ago in western Europe.

CHAPTER ONE:
THE LION CUB WAITS

Just before dawn on a cold spring morning, the wind came up in the river valley where Anooka and her clan lived. It prowled around the family hut, then entered with a whine through the cracks in the mud that sealed the wood and skins together. Anooka burrowed deeper under her bison night-robe. The wind tangled in her dream and became the whimpering of a lion cub.

Something rough touched her face. She opened her eyes to see her father squatting on his heels beside her.

Tor patted her cheek again. "Anooka, get up! You have a job to do today."

She didn't move. "I was dreaming. You woke

me up just before a mother lion comes back to her cub."

"You don't know that she'll return," he said.

"It's *my* dream—she'll come back!"

Tor's head was close to hers. "A mother lion can be cruel. If food is scarce, she'll feed herself and let her little ones go hungry." He broke off, his mouth a thin line, and said no more.

In the tense silence Anooka heard short bursts of laughter and the murmur of excited conversation outside the hut. She sat up. "It's still dark—why is everyone awake?"

"During the night the Salmon Spirit called the fish back to our river," he said.

Anooka scrambled to her feet. "The first salmon run! Why didn't you tell me?"

Tor turned his head away. "Because you're not going to the river today."

"Everyone who can goes to the river on the first day of the run!" Anooka cried out. "Aren't I a part of the Salmon Clan?"

"Yes, but you don't do the work of a Salmon Clan woman," he said. "I told you to help your sister with the first cleaning of the bearskin. But you were nowhere to be found while Nomi spent days on her knees hunched over that hide—alone. Now the second cleaning must be done."

"I'll do it tomorrow!" she pleaded.

"The bearskin is too thick and valuable to risk

damage by another night's freeze," Tor said. "But this is the *first* run," Anooka said. "I don't want to miss it!"

Tor stood and threw aside the hut's deerskin flap. "The Salmon Spirit and the fish keep their own time—not yours." He left.

Anooka started to call out to him but let the cry stop in her throat. She didn't want anyone to know what had happened between them.

With tears in her eyes Anooka sat slumped on her night-robe. She searched under the fur to find the ivory pendant she always held when falling asleep. Anooka had discovered it buried in the dirt floor of the hut long ago. She had told no one of the pendant, sure that her mother had left it behind.

Anooka held the delicate piece next to her face, then traced with a fingertip the three circles etched into its surface; each circle was ringed by two outer circles. Her constant touch was beginning to rub the ivory smooth. She longed to make something as beautiful, but it was the way of the Salmon Clan that only men could carve.

Leaves crunched outside the hut. Anooka quickly returned the pendant to its secret place under her robe, then reached for her tunic.

Her sister came in, a troubled look on her usually open and tranquil face.

"You were up early," Anooka said. "Did you come back to get your fish knife?"

Nomi avoided Anooka's gaze. "I couldn't find it in the dark."

Her sister was fifteen, only three years older than Anooka, but already a woman. Her deerskin trousers were tucked into boots that came up to her knees. She wore a fur-lined parka she had recently made. Its loose hood framed her face and set off her high cheekbones.

Anooka felt the flicker of envy—Nomi was beautiful. Tight braids circled her sister's head. When Nomi turned away to look for the knife, Anooka tried to smooth back her own thick and unruly hair. The gesture was useless.

"Father won't let me go to the river," Anooka said.

"I know." Nomi's tone was comforting. "I spoke for you, but he won't change his mind. There will be fishing trips until fall."

"But this is the first salmon run, the *best* day," Anooka cried out. "I don't want to be left behind."

Nomi shook her head. "Father gives you no choice. Come—he's waiting for us to help him attach the hide to the frame." She tucked the flat knife into her boot.

Anooka noticed a black design on the boot top. "Where did you get the idea to do that?"

"I loved to watch Mother make clothes," Nomi said, her voice turning slow and dreamy. "The other night, when I started the fire, I suddenly remembered her putting a sharpened stick into the flames, then burning a design onto the front of a tunic she was making. I did the same."

Anooka peered at the design. "It looks like two flying geese. Why did you choose them?"

"Geese are strong in flight," Nomi said. "They mate for life, and they follow the seasons together."

"Oh, Nomi—do you really want to marry?" Anooka said. "What if you don't like the man Father picked out for you at the last Gathering?"

"I trust Father to find a good husband for me." Nomi spoke forcefully, emphasizing every word.

Anooka shrugged. "I'm glad I'm not old enough to be married off. I don't want to think about being someone's wife . . . having to go to *his* clan to live."

"Well, I do, and your turn will come!" Nomi started to leave. "Hurry—Father hates to be kept waiting."

Anooka slowly tied back her tangled hair with a strip of leather, put on her trousers and boots, and started to take down the skin parka that Nomi had made for her last summer. It was so worn and stained that she left it hanging on the hook despite the morning cold.

Anooka squared her shoulders and walked past the six other huts set among the trees that bordered the camp clearing. Apart from her own family, there were twenty-eight people in the

Salmon Clan. Today their mood was festive. The three mothers with babies were getting out their back slings. Two men and their older sons bound braided sinew to their harpoons. Four excited young boys shouted and threw imaginary harpoons at each other.

"Got you!"

"No, you missed."

"I'm the best!"

"No, I am!"

Anooka hurried past five girls, all younger than herself, who were helping their mothers pack food into shoulder pouches for the long day ahead. One girl looked up. "Anooka, aren't you coming to the river?"

Quickly shaking her head, Anooka walked through the commotion until she reached the clearing. The bearskin lay stretched out on the ground. Her father stood beside it, his arms folded over his chest. Nomi crouched over the hide removing the wooden pegs that had kept it taut during the first cleaning.

Anooka felt her face blush with shame as she noticed Nomi's rough, red hands and jagged fingernails that came from scraping gobs of fat, flesh, and congealed blood from the underside of the bearskin. "I should have helped you, Nomi," she said under her breath. "I found a fox den full of pups and kept going back to watch them play."

"What took you so long?" her father's harsh voice broke in. "Some have started for the river."

Without answering, Anooka knelt beside Nomi. Together they took out the remaining pegs, then rolled up the icy skin. Tor lifted it to his shoulder and carried it to the standing frame he had set up at the outer edge of the clearing.

Anooka shivered without her parka. "Why so far from the hearth?"

Tor dropped the bearskin next to the frame. "When the sun warms the hide, those left in camp will not welcome the smell."

In silence they laced short strips of sinew through the peg holes, then lifted the hide and secured it to the frame with the strips. The bearskin was stiff and heavy, and their cold hands made the job even harder.

"I've made you a new scraper," Tor said, handing Anooka a blunt-edged flint tool. He opened his waist pouch and took out onion bulbs and a piece of dried deer meat. He offered them to her on his outstretched palm.

"I don't want food," Anooka said. "I want to go to the river!"

The muscles of her father's jaw clenched. He shoved the food back into his pouch and walked away.

Nomi waved as she hurried to catch up with

the fishing party. Anooka waved back weakly, her hand held low. With tears blurring the bearskin in front of her, she felt as abandoned as the cub in her dream.

CHAPTER TWO:
SINGING ON THE RIVERBANK

Anooka roughly wiped away her tears with the back of her hand. *I'll go to the river in spite of Father!* When she imagined his angry look on seeing her on the bank, she changed her mind. Anooka lifted the scraper and pressed it hard against the underside of the hide, repeating the motion over and over again.

She heard voices coming toward the clearing. Embarrassed to be in camp instead of at the river, Anooka kept herself hidden behind the bearskin as she worked.

Two men carried on a rumbling conversation as they settled by the fire. Anooka recognized their voices. One man had strained his back lifting a heavy deer carcass. The other had a wound in his leg from the tusks of a boar. Anooka soon heard the familiar sound of flint spear points being sharpened with chisels of antler.

A mother and her noisy little son arrived. The boy had outgrown a back sling, but would be too hard to manage on the riverbank without one.

Dragging steps moved slowly toward the hearth. Anooka peeked around the hide to see Owl sit close to the fire. As the old woman had aged, people began to call her by the name of the bird she resembled. Soon her beaky nose was close to two pieces of deerskin she was stitching together. Anooka ducked behind the bearskin before Owl could pierce her with a suspicious look from under her bushy white eyebrows.

Were the people around the fire talking about her? Anooka shut them out by concentrating on the hide. She worked without stopping through half the morning. The scraping was monotonous, and her thoughts drifted to the fishing party far away. The men and boys would be standing in the shallows of the river harpooning the salmon. After the writhing fish were heaved onto the shore, they would be scaled, gutted, and boned by the women and girls who waited on the slippery riverbank.

Under her breath, Anooka began to sing her favorite fishing song:

"Salmon, come to us gleaming—
Struggle against the river flow.
Salmon, come to us teeming—
Struggle against the river flow.
Come to us, come to us—
Come to us again."

A strong, soaring voice mysteriously joined in the song, and the radiant image of a young, black-haired woman came to Anooka. The singer had Nomi's high cheekbones and wide, smooth forehead, but Anooka thought her even more beautiful. The woman's oily fish knife flashed in the sun as she sang on the river-bank. Then Anooka saw in her mind's eye a little girl with thick, auburn hair who was hanging on to the long leather fringe of the woman's tunic.

Then she knew. *I'm that child! That's my mother!*

Anooka felt lightheaded. Her sudden memory was both painful and full of wonder. She didn't want it to disappear.

A high-pitched buzzing close to her ears brought Anooka back to the present. The pungent odor of the thawing bearskin had attracted a swarm of small, black flies. Most of them clustered on the hide's moist underside, but some flew close to her eyes. She waved them off, but they returned immediately.

13

Yearning to be at the river and maddened by the flies, Anooka tightened her grip on the flint scraper. She angled her tool steeply into the hide—a slicing sound! The force of her stroke had driven the blade through the bearskin. Anooka sucked in her breath. She furtively peered around the hide to see if her mistake had been noticed by the others.

It had.

Owl's bone needle had stopped in midair. "Now you've ruined it! Don't you know how valuable that hide is?"

"Anooka, pay attention to what you're doing," the young mother's voice rang out. "How will your father find you a good husband if you're so careless?"

The men ignored her and continued their lazy talk of hunting.

She knew where Nomi kept her sewing pouch. She also knew that her sister prized her tools and would not want her to use them. Anooka hesitated—Nomi was at the river. With her head down, Anooka hurried to the hut, found the pouch, and returned to the bearskin.

Anooka took out the flint awl that her father had made for her sister and did what she had seen clanwomen do all her life. She carefully worked the pointed tool back and forth into the hide, drilling two parallel rows of small holes on either side of the tear. She threaded Nomi's bone needle with thin fiber and painstakingly laced the holes together.

With the mending finished, Anooka walked around to the furry side of the hide. She smiled—it was impossible to tell where the gash had been.

Now the day stretched endlessly ahead. Anooka was hungry. Her right hand and shoulder ached. The flies clouded around her so thickly that she had given up trying to wave them off.

Toward midday a movement among the trees at the far side of the clearing caught her eye. A man was walking toward the hearth. Long before she saw his gray-streaked hair, she knew it was Durgun, shaman to the Salmon Clan. His graceful dancer's stride belied his years. Only Owl was older than Durgun.

Why was he here? Anooka could tell by the muttering of the people around the fire that they were asking each other the same question. The shaman rarely left his isolated hut, and she could not remember a time when he had let himself be seen on the day of the first salmon run. His appearance came later in the night.

Durgun came up to the frame and handed Anooka a small packet. "This will stop the ache in your stomach," he said quietly, "but not the one in your heart."

Moved at Durgun's concern for her, Anooka smiled her thanks. She looked inside the bundle and found the deer jerky and onions that she had refused earlier.

His face was grave. "Your father stopped on his way to the river and told me what had happened between you. He did not like leaving you behind."

Anooka shook her head. "Father finds fault with everything I do!" She lowered her voice when she saw that the people around the hearth were staring. "We're always quarreling—we'll never change."

"People are like the river—always changing," he said in a low, intense voice.

As she waited for him to continue, Anooka noticed that his face was moist with sweat and his breathing was heavy.

Durgun turned from her and looked closely at the bearskin. He fingered the mended gash. "Did Owl help you with this?"

"No, I didn't want her help," Anooka said.

"Your spirit is strong, Anooka, but you have many woman skills to learn," he said. "Let your sister teach you what you have to know while she's still here."

"Nomi would like that, but I wouldn't," Anooka said. "Once she's married, she'll have daughters of her own she can teach."

"Your tone of voice tells me that you have a distaste for such things," Durgun said.

Anooka felt embarrassed at being found out,

but also relief that Durgun had grasped her feelings. "There must be another kind of life I could live . . . something important I could do."

"What could be more important?" Durgun didn't wait for an answer. "All living things follow patterns, Anooka. When to leave the nest or den . . . or hut. When to mate. When to bear babies. We need children to maintain the clans." His voice dropped. "We need young people to care for us when we are sick and old . . . to remember us after we journey to the Spirit World."

"But you chose not to marry—you have no children," Anooka said, unable to stop herself. The blood rushed to her cheeks on hearing her disrespectful words.

"I did not choose," Durgun said sharply. "The Spirits did." He turned the right side of his face toward Anooka.

She wanted to close her eyes but could not. Claw marks had raked Durgun's face long ago. The wounds had healed, but one side of his mouth drooped and one eye stared open.

"The Spirits have created a life for me that is better lived alone," Durgun said in a lighter tone. "As for children, the clanpeople are my children." He touched her gently on the shoulder. "You and I have talked long enough—this bearskin is far from finished." He started to leave.

Anooka reached toward his arm, but stopped herself. She tried to hold him back with words.

"If the clanpeople are your children, then my mother was one of them. Durgun, I remembered her for the first time this morning. And I was with her . . . so young I could barely walk. Mother was singing . . . she seemed happy . . ." Anooka's voice trailed off.

Durgun had turned slowly to face her, his right eye unblinking. He said nothing.

"Father gets angry when I ask about Mother," Anooka said in a new rush of words. "Once in a while Nomi will remember some small thing, but she was only five when Mother left. No one else talks about her."

Again Durgun was silent.

"Talk to me about my mother!" Anooka said in a voice so strong that she worried the people at the hearth could hear her.

Durgun brushed his forehead lightly with his fingers. It was the clan gesture for a promise made. "Some things should not be talked about," he said, his scarred lips hardly moving.

He turned abruptly and walked toward his hut beyond the clearing. His dancer's step was gone.

CHAPTER THREE:
BEARS

Brooding over Durgun's words, Anooka returned to scraping the hide. Even the disappearance of the flies in the cooling afternoon did not lighten her mood.

The shadows were lengthening when she heard the return of the fishing party. By the lively talk and laughter, she knew the day on the river had been successful. Anooka put down her scraper and came from behind the bearskin to see the people straggling up the path laden with fish, knives, and harpoons.

Nomi trudged to the clearing with four salmon hanging from a sinew rope slung over her shoulder. She put down her load, then walked to the frame. "The river was teeming, 'Nooka. I wish you'd been with us."

Anooka touched her sister's braids. "You have fish scales in your hair. Like Durgun, you'll glisten in the firelight tonight."

Nomi smiled. "But only one of us will dance." She bent to look closely at the bearskin. "I didn't know you could mend like that."

"I wasn't sure I could." Anooka paused, then picked up the sewing pouch. "I borrowed this."

Nomi took the pouch with a quick motion. "It's time you had one of your own."

"I don't want one," Anooka said.

"*All* clanwomen have sewing pouches," Nomi said. "You reek of bear. Go wash while there's still some sun on the water."

Anooka was eager to be alone at the river, but knew she must wait for her father's inspection of her work.

Tor entered the clearing with ropes of salmon hung from both shoulders. He added them to the growing fish pile before coming to the frame. He grunted softly as he inspected the bearskin. Although his hand lingered over the mended tear, he made no comment on it.

Finally he spoke. "Durgun's night-robe is worn and gives little warmth. This will make a fine gift for him." He turned away from her. "Your work is finished. I'll take down the hide."

Proud that the bearskin would go to Durgun,

Anooka started for the river with her head high. "It will be dark soon," Nomi called out to her. "Don't go too far."

"I can take care of myself!" Anooka shouted over her shoulder.

On the riverbank Owl's two grandsons yelled and laughed as they splashed each other. Seeking privacy, Anooka walked on. Her steps were so light that a fish hawk hovering above the river took no notice of her. She caught her breath at the hawk's sharply angled dive into the water to catch its prey.

Anooka continued downriver until she found a shallow, sunny spot for her bath. Her boots were off when a low snort made her look up.

A thin brown bear not more than two years old sat in the river just ahead. Quickly looking around for its mother, Anooka was relieved when she could not find her. She was probably nursing the season's new cubs after chasing off this young one to fend for itself. Anooka ducked down behind some reeds to watch.

The bear thrashed around in the river, then rose up to slap the water clumsily with its paws. Anooka had watched bears fish in the river for as long as she could remember and knew this was a poor imitation of the fishing style of older bears.

With another snort the young bear clambered up to a little spit of land that jutted out into the river. It swatted the water again, but could not keep its balance. It slipped and slid and looked so confused that Anooka laughed. With a startled glance in her direction, the bear lurched from the peninsula, plunged into the trees, and disappeared.

Why would a sure-footed animal behave like that? She walked out onto the spit of land and found herself struggling to keep her own footing. Carefully she bent to touch the slick, finely grained soil beneath her bare feet. When she planted a foot deeper into the muck, it squished up between her toes. Anooka scooped up some of the slippery soil and cautiously left the peninsula for the firm ground of the riverbank.

What she held in her hand did not feel like the mud she and Nomi used to seal the cracks in the walls of their hut. When Anooka squeezed it between her fingers, water oozed out. She played with the heavy clump for a moment, then rolled it into a ball between her palms.

Shadows on the river made her suddenly aware of the time. She put the ball and her clothes on a rock that still held the warmth of the sun, then waded into the cold river. She ducked under the water and vigorously ran her hands over her skin and through her hair to get rid of the smell of bearskin. Anooka got out shivering, shook herself off, and quickly dressed. She picked up the little ball. It had hardened slightly.

Anooka made an indentation in the ball, the

top portion smaller than the bottom. A head and body appeared. She felt uneasy—the women of the Salmon Clan did not carve. Was this carving? She glanced nervously over her shoulder.

Thinking of the young bear, she began to shape its likeness with her fingers. How could she capture the bear's confused expression? How had it held its head? Its paws? She easily corrected the mistakes she made by smoothing them away and starting again. How different from her father's flint work or Durgun's ivory carving.

Ignoring the time and the cold, Anooka worked on. The sun was hidden behind the trees when she finished her piece. The bear was as thin and awkward as the one she had watched. She felt its loneliness and worried whether it would have the skills to survive by itself.

Anooka started back to camp holding the bear protectively in both hands. She skirted the clearing where preparations for the feast had begun. The family hut was empty. She hid the damp little bear in a cobwebby spot near the smoke hole in the roof.

Secrets, too many secrets. She thought of what Durgun must know about her mother. He had accrcto, too.

CHAPTER FOUR:
THE DANCE OF THE SALMON SPIRIT

Anooka hurried to the clearing. Near the hearth a shallow fire pit had been dug and lined with hot stones. Five large salmon stuffed with grassy herbs and green onions lay on top of the stones. She helped cover the fish with moss and bark to keep the heat from escaping. The good smells of roasting fish and onions brought people around the pit to wait and talk. It was almost dark by the time the women removed the baked salmon.

The feasting began. Tor sat among the men near the hearth. The boys sprawled together to eat. One after another they stood to throw their fish bones into the fire as if they were harpoons. The young girls sat in a group, giggling among themselves. The women gathered together to talk and eat after everyone had been served.

Anooka stood off to one side, unsure if she should sit with the girls or the women.

"Eat with us," Nomi called out.

All the women except Owl welcomed her with nods and smiles as she sat next to her sister. Anooka yearned to join in their spirited conversation, but held back.

The babies were asleep in their back slings when Anooka heard the sound she'd been waiting for—the strumming of the singing bow.

Durgun entered the clearing chanting to the steady twang of the bow's single string. His face, hands, and legs were coated with a dark stain, so all that could be seen of him in the flickering firelight was his sacred cape. Made of fragile salmon skins sewn together, it was worn only on the night of the first salmon run. Because the cape had been newly greased with animal fat, the scales reflected the firelight and glistened like a fish in the river.

Durgun stood motionless in the center of the clearing for a long moment. Anooka grew uneasy—it seemed too long. Suddenly he hit himself in the chest with the bow and leaped into the air, his torso writhing like a salmon pierced by a harpoon.

Durgun whirled in a tight circle with his bow held above his head. He sang in a loud, wavering voice that did not seem to come from his distorted mouth:

"The Salmon Spirit lives with me, lives in me.
When I strum, the Spirit wakens.
When I dance, the Spirit sees me.
When I sing, the Spirit hears me.
We are the salmon people.
Yes, we are the Salmon Clan."

Everyone rose to join Durgun in the chant. Each group of singers—men, women, and children—came together, then separated in a shimmering pattern of repeated words and melody. Anooka alone was silent. She had always sung with the children, but tonight she was uncertain whether she should sing with them or the women.

The intensity of the song increased with each swooping, driving refrain. Durgun's cape flowed out around him as he whirled in rhythm to the chant. In perfect balance he both led the clanpeople and was led by them.

When the singing was at its most powerful, Durgun stopped turning. Again he stood very still—Anooka's heart seemed to stop with him. The chanting ceased. Suddenly the shaman threw his bow into the air, caught it, and ran toward the fire. He leaped through the flames, then vanished into the darkness beyond the clearing.

Utter stillness. Then the clanpeople stirred as if awakening from a trance. Quietly they started back to their huts. Anooka felt that she was floating, not walking, toward home.

In the dark family hut Nomi was already under her robe. Anooka was pulling off her tunic when her father came in.

"The work you did on the bearskin was good, Anooka," he said. "These skills will be valued by your future husband and his clan."

She tried to steady her voice. "What if I don't want to marry?"

"What are you saying?" Tor said sharply. "You have no choice."

"Didn't Mother choose when she left?" Anooka asked.

"Anooka!" Nomi said in a choked voice.

Even though her body was rigid with worry, Anooka persisted. "Father, do you think she's dead?"

"She's dead to us, *dead to us!*" he said with icy anger.

Anooka and her father said no more to each other, but she was sure she was not the only sleepless one in the quiet hut. She held the pendant next to her cheek as her mind raced. She knew that tomorrow she must help with the smoking and storing of the salmon that had been caught today. But then she would visit Durgun to plead with him to talk to her about her mother.

CHAPTER FIVE:
CHEE-BOY

Nine slanted racks were already in place over hot embers when Anooka came to the clearing the next morning. She knew that her father and the other men had risen before dawn to make the racks and light the fires so the hard firewood could turn to charcoal for the long, slow smoking.

Tor was kneeling on the ground binding together the joints of another rack. He did not look up at her.

Anooka joined the women who were removing the branches and stones that had kept the catch safe from predators during the night. She bent to take the first of many loads of salmon to the racks. Stooping, lifting, carrying—the work did not let up all morning. No one stopped for the midday meal but instead ate pieces of crisp salmon that clung to the racks.

When the fish were smoked dry and cool enough to handle, Anooka helped wrap them in deerskin before stacking them in cold, deep underground pits. After every successful fishing trip the task would be repeated. Only with storage pits full of dried salmon could the clan remain camped by the river throughout the year and give up their old life of hunting and gathering.

When the storing of the fish was finished, Anooka's day was her own. She left the clearing and quickly walked beyond it to the pine forest. She was fearful she would lose her nerve and turn back if she slowed down. No one visited the shaman uninvited.

Her footsteps made crunching sounds as she searched among the cones and needles to find the path to Durgun's small hut. When it became visible ahead of her, half hidden beneath the pines, she walked toward it as silently as she could.

Durgun sat outside his low dwelling, his legs crossed beneath him and his head bowed. Although the height of the trees kept the forest in deep shade, shafts of sunlight filtered between the branches and fell on the shaman. Anooka's skin prickled. The Animal Spirits must

be here with Durgun in this dense forest. He must have heard her or sensed her, but she was not acknowledged.

"I have come unbidden to you," Anooka said quietly. Durgun looked up without surprise and gestured for her to sit opposite him. He held a small piece of ivory in one hand, a flint chisel in the other.

"What are you carving?" she asked.

Durgun did not raise his head. "Horse." His strokes were quick and sure, and made with such concentration that he seemed to shut out the world. Anooka leaned forward to watch him make tiny rows of scratch marks that became a furry winter coat on the horse's flanks, legs, and chin.

"I wish I could do that," Anooka said.

Durgun held up the little horse. "Ivory is sacred—now more than ever, for the Mammoth Spirit is calling home the beasts that carry the sweeping tusks." He returned to his etching. "You know that only men may carve. It is the way of the clan."

Having no answer to the clan's ways, Anooka was silent.

"You did not come here to talk about carving," Durgun finally said.

She clutched the pendant she had brought to give herself courage. "You make the salmon return to our river. If my mother lives, can you make her return to our clan?"

His hands stopped moving. "I am in touch with the Animal Spirits. I help heal the human body. But the human heart is mysterious and difficult to control."

Anooka tried to blink back sudden tears. "I come to you because you know things I must know. No one has even spoken my mother's name to me."

Without looking up, Durgun shook his head. "I told you I cannot talk of her."

"You must—there is no one else I can turn to!" Anooka's strong voice became whispery. "Why did Mother leave?"

Because Durgun was silent, she would tell him her deepest fear. "I've always thought I made her go away."

He looked at her, staring. "Why do you think that?"

Anooka steadied herself. "Nomi must have been a good child, beautiful, uncomplaining . . . so I must have been the one to make her go." She looked away. "Maybe I was too whiny, not pretty enough . . ."

"Oh, Anooka, you did nothing, nothing. I never imagined you would blame yourself." Durgun seemed to struggle before continuing. "Lulaq was your mother's name. She loved both you and Nomi . . . as she loved the baby that came after you."

Anooka gasped. "A baby! I don't remember a baby."

"You were too young," Durgun said. "It was a boy—named Chee. Your father called him Chee-boy. That baby brought much grief to the clan."

She turned cold. "What happened?"

"Shortly after the baby's naming ceremony, Lulaq put Chee in her back sling and went to collect reeds for his cradle." His voice was low and breathy. "She hung the sling high on a nearby branch and went off in search of the softest reeds. At the river's edge Lulaq heard his cry and rushed back. The sling lay on the ground— bloody, torn, and empty."

"Empty?" Anooka echoed.

"Leopard probably . . . Chee's body was never found," Durgun said. "At his funeral ceremony the earth received only a little fur cape from Lulaq and a tiny harpoon from Tor."

Tears spilled down Anooka's cheeks, but she didn't make a sound.

"Some few days after the funeral, your father returned to his hut and found Lulaq and all her possessions gone."

Not all. Anooka gripped the pendant so hard that it hurt her hand. "Why did she go away?"

He shifted uneasily. "Your mother was a skilled and inventive woman who came from a clan that prized these traits. When she married your father, she refused to leave her old clan's ways behind."

"What were these ways?" Anooka asked.

"Lulaq's clothes were beautifully decorated; her baskets were tight and wonderfully woven," Durgun said. "Some of the women resented her skills, but your mother was indifferent to their feelings and would not change. After Chee was killed, they treated her cruelly and persuaded their families to do the same."

"What do you mean?" Anooka asked.

"They blamed her for leaving the baby unattended," he said.

"Blamed her?" she cried out. "They should have comforted her!"

Durgun reached out and held her shoulder for a moment. "I tried to comfort her . . . as did others. Lulaq came to me after Chee's death to talk about her loss, Tor's loss. . . . He had wanted a son, of course."

Of course. Anooka felt a flash of resentment.

"Your mother would not be comforted," Durgun said with resignation. "I spoke to all who judged her harshly and tried to change their minds. I succeeded with some—but not enough. The quarrels were bitter."

Anooka thought of the harsh old woman. "Owl blamed her, didn't she?"

Durgun looked away.

"Father never speaks of her, so he must have blamed her, too," Anooka said.

"Listen to me!" Durgun's voice shot up. "No one in the clan is allowed to talk about the baby's death or Lulaq's disappearance."

"But Chee was my brother—Lulaq my mother!" Anooka said.

"A vow was taken long ago," Durgun said. "After your mother left, the people who had judged Lulaq harshly were blamed for her leaving. People turned on one another. The turmoil grew—our clan was tearing itself apart. To preserve and heal the clan, the adults came together and pledged never to speak of these events again."

"But you've spoken to me," Anooka said. "What made you break your vow?"

The lines in Durgun's face were deeper; his forehead was furrowed as if he were in pain. "I could not let you carry a burden that is not yours."

Anooka wanted to embrace him but dared not. "Thank you, Durgun," she whispered. "One last question—do you think my mother lives?"

He raised his shoulders, then dropped them. "No one knows. . . . She did not return to her old clan. For days search parties went out—she left no traces. Lulaq was resourceful, but she walked away without weapons or hunting skills."

A wave of exhaustion wrapped around Anooka.

Slowly she held out her hand and opened her fingers to reveal the pendant.

"Ah," Durgun said in a drawn-out sigh. "I never expected to see this again." He ran his fingers over the ivory. "I carved this for Lulaq just after Chee's birth. The design was hers."

"What does it mean?" Anooka asked, thinking of Nomi's geese.

"The three inner circles stood for her three children. The outer circles stood for their growth, their blossoming. . . ." He returned the pendant to her with wet eyes.

Anooka rose. Durgun had given her something more valuable than the pendant—the truth. She bowed her head to the shaman and left.

CHAPTER SIX:
SISTERS

Anooka no longer saw the beauty of the dark forest as she walked away from Durgun's hut. She stumbled over pine cones and slipped on dry pine needles as her thoughts whirled in her head. A brother she could not remember was dead. Her mother had refused to fit into the life of a Salmon Clan woman. Had she been strong or foolish? Was her mother dead? Was this the price one paid for being a different kind of woman?

She was near the river when she heard the distant twang of Durgun's bow. She listened to the sad music, and all her sorrows came together. She wept as she walked, unsure whether her tears were for Chee, for her mother's suffering, or for herself.

She stopped to splash cold water on her swollen eyes and realized she was near the spit of land where she had found the strange mud. Carefully she walked out onto the peninsula, then squatted to run her hands over the smooth surface. She gathered a lump of the moist earth, wrapped it in leaves, and put it in her shoulder pouch.

Anooka came upon Nomi filling her water skin at the riverbank on the path back to camp. Her sister started to greet her, but stopped. "What's wrong?"

Anooka did not reply.

Nomi stood. "Stop staring at me—what is it?"

"I went to Durgun's hut to find out about Mother."

Nomi's eyes grew round. "You did *what?*"

"Durgun talked to me about her, about the baby I'm sure you remember," Anooka said. "You should have told me long ago!"

Nomi held the half-filled water skin to her chest as if for protection. "Father told me never to talk about Mother or Chee."

Anooka stepped closer. "Every adult in the clan must know about them. You've kept this from me . . . as if I were a child."

"You act like one—a child who thinks she's the only one to lose a mother!" Nomi shot back.

Anooka was shaken by Nomi's anger. "When fall comes, you'll leave and be done with me."

40

"True," Nomi said through tight lips. She swung around to go.

Anooka grabbed her arm. "Who will I talk to when you're gone?"

"We used to talk," Nomi said. "We haven't for a long time."

"Talk to me now." Anooka sat down and patted the ground beside her. "Tell me about Mother and the baby."

Letting the water skin drop to her side, Nomi quickly looked up and down the riverbank. "I've kept my memories hidden for so long that sometimes I think I've made them up."

"Tell me what you remember," Anooka pleaded.

"I remember the baby," Nomi said in her dreamy voice. "Thick, spiky hair. So little, just like the goatskin doll Mother made for me before he was born . . . I kept it until it fell apart. I remember Chee's naming day. Mother wore a tunic sewn with shells that came from the sea." Her gaze turned inward. "I remember how they caught the sunlight and shone."

"Durgun told me her clothes were different," Anooka said.

Nomi nodded. "At the baby's naming ceremony Durgun began a song of celebration for Chee's safe birth. Father joined in the chant and sang so loud that I became frightened and clung to Mother." Nomi crossed her arms over her chest as if she were holding a child to her shoulder.

41

"Mother couldn't pick me up because she was holding you, 'Nooka."

"Did Durgun hold Chee?"

"Yes, but the baby seemed to disappear in the folds of the little cape he was wrapped in—the fur was as black as his hair," Nomi said. "I asked Mother if he was really inside. When Chee began to whimper, Mother smiled down at me."

"Yesterday I remembered Mother for the first time," Anooka said. "She was singing on the riverbank . . . her hair as black and shiny as a raven's wing."

"You remember her well," Nomi said. "She sang all the time after Chee's birth. Even Father was full of smiles and laughter. And then"— Nomi closed her eyes—"everything changed."

"Yes," Anooka whispered, putting her arms around her sister.

They held and rocked each other.

"Let's go home," Anooka said.

While Nomi built up the fire in the hut, Anooka removed the dry, cracked mud along one wall of the hut.

"What are you doing?" Nomi asked.

Anooka took out the lump from her shoulder pouch and smoothed it into the wall. "I discovered this up the river—I think it will seal the hut better than the mud we've always used."

Nomi looked skeptically at the patches. "Why do you think it will be better?"

"I'll show you." Anooka brought her little bear down from its hiding place. "Feel how firm this is."

Nomi touched the figure on Anooka's outstretched palm. "This is good—but should you have made it?"

Tor entered the hut. "Made what? Let me see." He held out his hand.

Stiffly Anooka handed him the bear. He glared at her. "You did this?"

Anooka's mouth was dry. She nodded. He held up the piece. "You're like your mother—refusing the ways of the clan."

In one quick motion Anooka snatched back the bear and threw it into the fire. "There—I've killed it!" she shouted. "Are you happy, Father? Does this make me the kind of obedient daughter you can praise at the Gathering?"

She stormed out of the hut.

CHAPTER SEVEN:
THE SECRET CAVE

If I'm like Mother, Anooka said to herself, *I'll make another bear!*
Walking fast on the riverbank, she was surprised at how quickly she reached the little spit of land. Carefully Anooka walked out on the peninsula and gathered up a handful of the slippery clay.

She looked around for a secluded spot to work. A small ledge jutted out from the foothills that rose up close to the river. Clutching the clay in one hand, Anooka used the other to clamber up to the rocky projection.

There was a small opening in the hill just in back of the ledge. It looked like the entrance to a cave. It was a good den for a bear still in hibernation—a dangerous place for someone without a weapon. Anooka crouched on the ledge and sniffed the air for the rank, musky odor of bear. Smelling nothing but pine, she peered inside the opening.

The cave was empty. Anooka took a few hesitant steps inside. The rocky ceiling was low, but she could stand upright. Sunlight penetrated halfway into the interior, and the sandy floor was clean and undisturbed.

Anooka sat near the entrance and shaped her second bear with more assurance. Her hands remembered what they had learned from modeling the first one, and the new piece came to life beneath her fingers. She worked without stopping until the bear's shape and proportions satisfied her. But it lacked something. She scratched short, uneven strokes on the surface of the animal with her fingernail, and a coat of fur appeared. The bear, no bigger than her palm, was finished.

Anooka looked at her work with new eyes. This bear was different from the first one—not as thin and awkward, more robust and able to care for itself. She smiled at the bear, then put the moist piece next to the wall near the sunny entrance. Rubbing her clay-coated hands together, Anooka walked out on the ledge to stretch her cramped legs. The day was almost over and she hadn't eaten. She would bring food next time.

Filled with new energy, Anooka scrambled down from the ledge. At the halfway point to the riverbank, she stopped to look back. The cave could not be seen at all, and the ledge itself blended into the rocks and boulders of the foothills. She had found a safe place, a secret place.

Instead of hurrying on, Anooka looked at the river valley spread out before her. Her mother had once looked out on this same valley. The snow-topped mountains rose up protectively on either side. The blue-green river carried shimmering patterns of sunlight on its surface. She had never been so aware of the beauty that surrounded her—and that had once surrounded her mother.

The salmon were now coming to the river in great numbers. For days the entire clan worked together to smoke and store the fish. They would be eaten dry, added to stews, or coated with grease and grilled through the long wintry months ahead.

When the surge of salmon began to taper off, Anooka felt free to claim a day for herself. She set out for her cave, glancing back frequently to make certain no one was watching or following her.

A feather-crested spoonbill waded in the river close to the bank. The mysterious birds appeared only in the spring with the salmon runs. The spoonbill was searching for small fish and frogs so intently that Anooka could get close to study it.

Back in her cave, Anooka began to shape the spoonbill, but it would not emerge from her fingers. The legs of the bird had to be long and thin—too fragile to support its clay body. She worked most of the day trying to solve her problem, but gave up by the late afternoon. She reluctantly kneaded her bird back into a lump and returned to camp.

After three days of salmon smoking, Anooka went back to the cave carrying asparagus and sedge root in her shoulder pouch. For something to drink with her meal, she stopped by the river to fill an old, discarded water skin she had found.

She started to work again, but her hands could no longer move smoothly over the surface of the clay. She put the water skin by her side and eased the slide of her fingers on the piece by keeping them wet. She modeled the bird as if it were standing in the water, its legs concealed in a small platform of clay. By the end of the day her spoonbill looked like the one on the river, its head tilted, its watchful eyes wide.

Anooka yearned to show her pieces to someone—especially her mother. Would she be proud of her daughter for doing something different?

Anooka was careful not to be absent from camp for more than one day out of many.

47

Although she helped in the work of the clan without being asked, she saw suspicion in her father's eyes. They rarely spoke to each other when they met on the river or while preparing the salmon. Their silence was even more awkward in the family hut at the beginning and end of the day.

One afternoon, when the sisters were alone in the hut, Nomi asked, "Where do you go when you're away from camp?"

"To a place that makes me happy," Anooka said.

"Be careful," Nomi said. "Father has noticed your absences."

Anooka's cave gradually became a place of work. She gathered and kept her clay in an old, cast-off basket. To cushion her knees, she knelt on a worn piece of fur as she worked. A square slab of stone served as a platform for her modeling. Her bear and bird sat on a piece of bark balanced on two flat rocks.

Her next piece would be based on a long-ago memory. When Anooka was a little girl, her father had brought her a fat wolf pup to admire. She'd stroked its soft fur while he cradled it in his arms, one hand holding its mouth shut to keep the pup's sharp teeth from nipping her.

She began to shape the wolf, but even with wet hands she found the clay had become too dry to work at all. With a groan she returned the clay into the basket. Then Anooka added water and kneaded the clay and water together. It was hard work, but the clay gradually softened. At the end of the day, a bowlegged wolf pup with folded ears and a little twig of a tail joined the little bear and spoonbill on the bark shelf.

The next day she and Nomi stood together cutting up salmon for smoking. Without missing a stroke, Nomi said, "Father keeps asking me where you go."

"Don't tell him, but I found a little cave way up the river where I go to make little animals," Anooka whispered. "Come and look at them."

Nomi shook her head. "Keep your secrets, Anooka. I'm worried that Father will sense that I know where you go and what you do."

"But I don't want to keep secrets from you," Anooka said.

"People have a way of finding out things," Nomi said. "You were able to make Durgun talk about the past. And Owl noticed the new design on my boots yesterday." Nomi's voice became peevish as she mimicked Owl. " 'Women of *this* clan do not call attention to themselves by decorating their clothes.' "

Anooka covered her mouth to muffle her laughter.

But Nomi quickly became serious. "What

you're doing in your cave is worse than burning a design on boots."

"Worse? You told me you liked my little bear."

"What I like has nothing to do with it!" Nomi said in a voice loud enough to make two women working nearby look in her direction.

"Hush," Anooka said under her breath.

Some days later Anooka woke up to a gray morning. Nomi sat in front of a small fire braiding her hair. They were alone. Anooka got down the bison horn her father took on hunting trips and removed the wooden plug that covered its opening. She scooped up hot embers from the hearth with a bone spoon, slid them into the horn, and replaced the plug.

"You're going to build a fire in your cave, aren't you?" Nomi said.

Anooka nodded. "When the sun doesn't shine, the cave is cold and damp." She slung the horn's strap over her shoulder and left.

As she walked toward the cave, Anooka collected moss and kindling for her fire and rocks to circle her hearth. Once there she took out the dry moss, and placed it in her new hearth. When she poured hot embers from the bison horn on top of the tinder, curls of thin smoke rose up. Tendrils of flame appeared after she blew on the embers.

Anooka added kindling, then sat back on her heels and smiled. *It's my fire, on my hearth, in my cave.*

Her reverie was shattered when she heard pebbles falling. The noise came closer. A creature was on the ledge. Anooka grabbed a piece of firewood and stood up with the branch gripped tightly in both hands.

CHAPTER EIGHT:
INTRUDER

The entrance darkened. Her father stood framed in the opening with his head lowered, his shoulders hunched.

Anooka's legs felt weak. To gain time, she turned away to add the wood she clutched to the fire. "Nomi told you about my cave, didn't she?"

"Nomi always protects you," Tor said. "She kept your secret—you did not."

"What do you mean?" Anooka asked.

"You lit a fire," he said. "But even before I saw the smoke, I've known you were in this area."

Anooka forced herself to breathe slowly and deeply. "How could you know this?"

"I'm a hunter," he answered. "I follow tracks . . . broken branches . . . the disturbed surface on a spit of land near here. A bit of tunic caught on a twig. You were not hard to track."

"You've hunted me down," Anooka said bitterly. Then she pointed to the fur piece. "My ceiling is too low for you—sit here."

Tor entered the cave and sat with a grunt, his legs crossed beneath him. He eyed the fire in the hearth, then his bison horn, which he pointedly took back. His gaze circled the cave as he looked at the stone platform, the water skin, and the basket filled with clay. He reached out to break off a small clump, then saw the figures on the bark shelf.

"You are disobedient!" he shouted, angrily throwing the clay into the fire as if it were unclean. "Durgun carves the Animal Spirits—you do not!"

"But no one has seen them," Anooka said in a pleading tone.

He seemed not to hear her. "I'm not responsible for the ways of the clan, but I am responsible for you!"

"You've come to forbid me to make my animals," Anooka said.

"That—and more," he said.

More?

"You are quick to anger," he continued. "In this cave, no one can hear us."

"I'm not soft-spoken like Nomi," Anooka said. "I know you wish I were more like her. She's happy about her marriage. . . ."

53

"Why shouldn't she be?" Tor said. "I've picked out a good man for her."

Anooka stared at her father. "Perhaps *Lulaq* found another way for a woman to live."

"Where have you heard this name?" he said in a voice cold with mistrust.

Anooka looked at her father, who was coiled like a snake ready to strike. He had found her cave. He had seen her animals. He would find out one more secret.

"Durgun has spoken to me about the past," she said.

Her father's eyes grew wide. "There was a vow taken—why would he do such a thing?"

"There was a vow made to heal the clan," she said, "not one to pretend my mother never existed."

"What did he tell you?"

"He spoke about Chee, about the quarreling among the clanpeople after he was killed," she answered.

"Chee-boy," Tor murmured.

Anooka wanted to comfort him, but would not. "He was my brother—how could you have kept all this from me? Now will you tell me why Mother left?"

He made a dismissive gesture with his hand. "I'm here to discuss the future, not the past."

She covered her ears. "You mean *my* future. I don't want to listen."

"You will hear me!" he said. "I want you married before people find out that you're likely to cause problems in your husband's clan. I will choose a man for you at the next Gathering."

"I'm too young!" Anooka shouted.

His hand sliced the air to silence her. "Your mother abandoned all her responsibilities—I will not!" He rose, almost hitting his head against the low ceiling. "Nor will you!"

CHAPTER NINE:
THE *TOC* CALL

Everything changed after her father's visit to the cave. Anooka's anger gradually turned into a dull sadness. She had planned to make a sleeping fox with its long, thick tail wrapped around its body. The fox did not find its place on the bark shelf, and the clay in the basket turned hard.

Anooka went often to the river as a member of the fishing parties, but the excitement that came with the first run was gone. Cleaning the harpooned fish was now wearisome work. She hardly spoke to anyone—certainly not to her father. She had not seen Durgun since she had visited him in his hut.

One morning Anooka decided to pay a rare visit to her cave to be alone in her ordered, private place. Halfway up to the ledge she stopped to look around her in the hope that she could feel again the beauty of the river and the surrounding mountains. The vivid green growth of spring was past, and blackberries had ripened into summer sweetness. She bent to pick the fruit. When she straightened up, strange flashes of light appeared in the distance. After a brief display they vanished.

A raven's distinctive *toc* call suddenly filled the air. It was not the bird's usual harsh cawing, but a short, hollow-sounding cry repeated over and over again. It was the call of a mother raven gathering her fledglings to her. Expecting to see birds circling above her, Anooka looked up. There were no ravens in the sky.

After a moment's silence the *toc toc toc* returned. Louder. The calls were coming from across the river. Drawn to them as if she had no choice, Anooka ran down the rocky hill heedless of the danger of falling.

She stopped only on reaching the bank. Across the river, small in the distance, a person sat on the far shore! The figure stood. It was a woman—her tunic almost touched the ground.

The stranger made a large, beckoning gesture with one hand. "Come to me," she called out.

Anooka stood rooted on her side of the bank, her mind a jumble of hope and apprehension. The swirling river flowed between them. With a burst of energy she did not understand, Anooka plunged into the water, which moved too rapidly for swimming. Within moments the water was up to her chest. The fast-moving current knocked her down. Her head went under as she struggled for secure footing. Sputtering and coughing, she came up almost out of breath.

She barely recovered her balance before falling again, but now she made herself move forward, forced herself to stay upright. Flailing her arms, Anooka fought her way across the river. She finally pulled herself onto the far shore by grabbing at the roots and reeds that grew along the bank. She stopped to gulp the air and sweep back her wet, tangled hair.

The regal figure stood quietly as if waiting for Anooka to appear before her. Only Durgun at the ceremonies was as striking. The woman's patterned tunic had been stitched together from various kinds of skin and fur. A knife of green flint was at her waist. Thin strips of white fox fur had been woven into the shiny black braids that circled her head. Her only movement was the light fingering of a string of carved ivory beads around her neck.

"Who are you?" Anooka said.

"I am RavenWoman," came the answer. "I was not always called this."

Anooka's heart was large in her chest. "What was your other name?"

"Lulaq," she answered.

"Lulaq was my mother," Anooka said, her voice strong. "She left so long ago that I thought she was dead."

The woman did not falter. "You see me here before you. I am Lulaq no longer—but still your mother." She moved forward and lightly ran the back of her hand over Anooka's cheek. "I only have to look at your face to know you are my daughter."

Anooka was weak with longing. "Have you come home to us?"

"No," RavenWoman answered. "I come but briefly."

No echoed in Anooka's heart. She wanted to throw her arms around her mother to prevent her from leaving. "Then why are you here?"

RavenWoman smiled at the same time her black eyes narrowed slightly. "Because it is time—you are no longer a child."

"Father will choose a husband for me soon," Anooka said.

"I've heard that he's started to make inquiries," her mother said. "And Nomi will go with her husband this fall."

Anooka took in her breath. "How do you know this?"

"Many people of the western clans go to your Gatherings to trade, to find husbands for their daughters, wives for their sons," RavenWoman said. "They return with news of alliances, disputes, marriages. I have kept track of you and Nomi for a long time." A softer, more motherly expression appeared on her face. "Is your sister happy with her coming marriage?"

"She welcomes it," Anooka said.

"And you?" she asked.

Anooka looked at the ground. "I was not asked what I wanted."

"And if you had been asked?" her mother persisted.

"I would refuse," Anooka said. "I want another kind of life."

RavenWoman leaned forward. "I'm here to offer you such a life—before it's too late, before you marry."

Anooka was filled with an explosive rage. "It's too late! How could you offer me anything now?"

"You are angry with me, of course," RavenWoman said. "But I think this anger has given you a kind of strength. The life I speak of demands determination. You showed this when you crossed that wild spot on the river to come to me."

Had this been a test? Anooka wondered. In spite of the danger of the crossing, Anooka felt a rush of pleasure at her mother's praise. "What kind of life do you offer me?"

"A life like mine." RavenWoman lifted her chin. "I am a healer, a medicine woman."

Anooka gazed at her mother with astonishment. "Are you a shaman . . . like Durgun?"

"Many think so," she answered. "My skills are celebrated among the western clans. In exchange for healing, I am given food and lodging, skins and furs, weapons and jewelry."

"How did you become a healer?"

"I used to watch Durgun when he performed his healing rites . . . so full of power and purpose," RavenWoman said. "I pleaded with him to tell me about his salves and potions. Gradually he shared some of his knowledge with me. Because of his generosity I had something I could offer the clans I encountered after I left my own." She spoke proudly. "Now I may know more than Durgun."

"More than the shaman of the Salmon Clan?" Anooka asked.

"Perhaps," she said. "I seek out the old ones in the clans I visit. I listen to their healing lore and learn from them. As I travel from clan to clan, I always look closely at growing things and remember what I see. If a fallen leaf remains on the forest floor free of mold or decay, it may possess a useful medicine. A plant avoided by insects may contain a substance helpful in warding off human sickness."

"You would share this knowledge with me?" Anooka asked.

RavenWoman put her hand lightly on Anooka's shoulder. "I would—it's time for you to be with your mother. If you join me, you will find that people will want you, wait for you, be grateful to you."

Her mother smiled at her, but Anooka, her mind reeling, did not smile back.

RavenWoman opened a woven grass pouch and took out a small deerskin packet wrapped in sinew. "A great hunter from the north sent for me after his chest was ripped open by the tusks of a mammoth. After I healed his wounds, he gave me this." She opened the packet to reveal a smooth black shard the size of her palm. When she handed it to Anooka, it flashed in the sun.

Was this what I saw glittering in the distance on my climb to the ledge? Anooka asked herself.

"Hold it close . . . look into it," her mother said.

Anooka had often gazed at herself in the still places of the river. Now, peering into the shiny rock, she saw her own face clearly for the first time. Slowly she touched her mouth, her forehead. Her high cheekbones. Her hand trembled as she returned the magical stone that she felt only a shaman could possess. "I see I am your daughter."

RavenWoman glanced at the sky. "The day is half over. I must start my long journey back to the western clans."

Longing and disappointment swept over Anooka. "Stay—I have so many questions to ask you."

63

Her mother cupped Anooka's face in her palms. "Join me—and I will answer them." Her expression grew somber. "You must vow to tell no one of our meeting who could prevent you from coming to me."

Anooka touched her forehead with her fingers. RavenWoman put her arms through the straps of her finely stitched leather backpack. Attached to it was a wooden bow like Durgun's, bedding, and a narrow reed pouch. When she flung her grass pouch over one shoulder, Anooka was startled by the glint of tiny sparks. Looking closely she saw that small beads of amber had been sewn into its woven grasses.

"How will we meet again if I decide to join you?" Anooka murmured.

"At the next full moon, I will be waiting where the west river forks before it gathers itself to surge into the sea." RavenWoman turned to leave. "Come to me, Anooka."

CHAPTER TEN:
TELLING NOMI

The last thing Anooka saw as her mother walked away from her was the sparkle of sunlight on amber beads. Her mother had returned, but as briefly as a raven that drops down to the forest floor and flies away moments later. But this raven had left something behind—an invitation to begin a new life of power and purpose.

Anooka shook herself out of her spell and hurried to the edge of the river. She found a spot where the water ran slowly and smoothly and swam to the other side. Back on the familiar side of the river, Anooka raced to the clearing, hoping to find Nomi there.

Her sister was sitting by the hearth sewing

and talking with three other women. Anooka caught Nomi's eye and beckoned to her.

Nomi walked toward her, an unfinished pouch of bleached white deerskin in her hand. Before being dried and softened, the skin had soaked for days in a bowl of urine just outside the hut. Anooka tried to imagine herself going to her husband's clan with newly made clothes, pouches, and baskets. She could not.

"'Nooka, you're wet," Nomi said.

"I must talk to you." Anooka took her arm. "Walk with me."

Anooka spoke only when she was sure they could not be overheard by the women. "Nomi, something happened this morning. I saw Mother!"

Nomi's eyes were round. "Mother—she's come home! Where is she? Take me to her!"

Anooka shook her head. "She's not returning to us—she's already started back to the western..."

"How could she go without seeing me?" Nomi interrupted with a strangled shout. "I don't believe it was Mother!"

Anooka's words tumbled out. "It was! She spoke our names . . . she's kept track of us for years. . . ."

"Why hasn't she come before?" Nomi asked, her gentle face distorted by hurt and anger. "She's never even sent a message to tell us she's alive."

"Nomi, she's changed." Anooka hesitated, sure

that whatever she said would be wrong. "She's an important healer now."

"I don't care what she is!" Nomi said. "Show me where you talked together!"

Anooka pointed across the river and Nomi raced to the bank. When Anooka caught up with her, her sister stood gazing at the opposite shore. "Now she's walked away from me twice," Nomi said bitterly.

Anooka reached out to touch Nomi's shoulder. "I know how much you've missed her."

Nomi shook free of her sister's hand. "I've lived most of my life without her. . . . I can continue."

Anooka realized there would be no good time to tell Nomi her news. "Mother wants me to join her."

Nomi stared at Anooka, her eyes hard. "So that's why she came."

"She will teach me to be a healer," Anooka said. "We will travel among the western clans together."

Nomi's voice shot up. "You will have no clan, no people of your own!"

"I want to be with her." Anooka's voice was shaky, not as powerful as she wanted it to be. "Father says I'm like her."

Nomi shook her head impatiently. "He says that when he's angry at you. Do you want to be like the woman who left us?"

Anooka tried not to show how shaken she was by what Nomi was saying. "Father is going to have me marry early. This is my chance to leave before he chooses a husband for me in the fall." She spoke as if she had no command over her words. "Mother must be a powerful shaman. You should have seen her clothes, her jewelry!"

"Durgun wears no jewelry," Nomi muttered through tight lips. "How are you supposed to find this person who's already on her way back to the western clans?"

"At the next full moon, she'll wait for me where the west river forks," Anooka said.

"What makes you so sure that she'll be there?" Nomi snapped.

"I know she'll be waiting," Anooka said in a tone she hoped sounded confident.

Nomi's stare was hard. "You have to speak to Father."

"Speak to Father?" Anooka gasped. "I can't. Mother made me promise not to tell anyone who could prevent me from joining her."

"I don't care what vow you took." Nomi said. "You must ask Father's permission to go."

"He'll refuse," Anooka said.

"Father has raised you by himself." Nomi's voice rose. "You owe him more than silence."

Anooka drew herself up. "If I'm old enough to marry, I'm old enough to make my own decision."

"I don't think you know what's right for you,"

Nomi said, glaring at her. "Not so long ago you were angry at me for keeping secrets from you. Now you're full of secrets. I didn't tell anyone about your cave or your animals. But I won't keep Mother's visit a secret—or what you're thinking of doing!"

CHAPTER ELEVEN:
THE SINGING BOW

The thought of returning to the hut to face her father's fury and her sister's contempt called for more courage than Anooka had. She went to her cave for consolation. Kneeling on the fur fragment without moving, her eyes unfocused, she stayed there for a long time. Anooka was stiff when she finally stood. She was unconsoled.

Mother went to Durgun for comfort, Anooka said to herself. *So will I.*

As she hurried toward Durgun's hut, only the shrill shriek of hawks and the distant yapping of a fox broke the silence of the pine forest.

Coming closer, Anooka found the skin flap of the hut open. She had never been inside and could not resist bending at the entrance to look. On the floor was a wooden tray that held Durgun's healing ointments and herbs. His bow hung high above the hearth, its burnished wood reflecting the flames of the little fire below. A loosely rolled skin lay on the floor, faint scales on its dull surface. Could this be the salmon-skin cape that had shimmered in the firelight?

The shaman lay motionless, facedown, under the bearskin robe her father had given him. She was sure he was asleep until she heard his wracking cough. Anooka crept into the hut.

"Durgun," she called softly.

He rolled over and struggled to sit up, but sank back with a soft moan.

"Are you sick?" Anooka asked. "Shall I go and get help?"

"Come and sit beside me—I've wanted to see you," Durgun said. His voice was shallow. Again he tried and failed to sit up. "Your father just left to look for a stand of willows far from here. Tea brewed from willow leaves lightens pain."

"You're in pain?" She knelt by his side. "Where?"

He touched his chest. "Here. The tightness is sharper now, but it's been with me for a long time."

Anooka suddenly remembered his sweaty forehead and labored breathing when he had come to the clearing to bring her food, his hesitations during the dance, and his creased brow when she had visited him outside his hut.

"You heal others," she said urgently. "You must heal yourself!"

"I've tried," Durgun whispered.

She bent over him. "You are powerful—the salmon come to our river because of you."

Durgun smiled slightly. "Perhaps they would come without my calling them." He waved away the discussion. "Your father will return—our time to be alone is short. There are important things for us to talk about."

"So many things," Anooka said softly.

"Let's start with the animal figures your father told me about."

"I shape them with my fingers out of a special mud I found," Anooka said, holding up her hands. "And I worked far from the clan in a secret cave—but Father found me."

"I'm glad he did . . . too many secrets," Durgun said. "Bring me one of your figures. I will think about what you are saying."

Anooka nodded. *Too many secrets*. She would be open with Durgun. "Father knows that I spoke to my mother this morning, doesn't he?"

"Yes, Nomi told him—and Tor came to tell me." Durgun paused. "At the Gatherings we have long heard about a healer called RavenWoman who goes among the western clans. It never occurred to us that this could be Lulaq."

Anooka turned away to add wood to the sputtering flames. "You must also know I'm thinking of joining her."

"Tor thinks RavenWoman has put you in a trance so she can steal you from us," Durgun said. "Your father will never let you go."

"But she's my mother," Anooka said, "and she's offered me a new kind of life—an important life."

"Your mother has no clan." Durgun sighed. "The life of a healer can be lonely."

Anooka looked down at the shaman, frail beneath the heavy bearskin. "Have you been lonely?"

In spite of her brash question, he met her gaze without irritation. "I have chosen to be apart and alone. I am seen at the ceremonies, then I return here to the pine forest." As he spoke, he absently ran his hand over the damaged side of his face.

"Durgun, people talk about your accident, but will you tell me about it yourself?" Anooka asked.

He drew a long breath. "When I was a young man, I was hunting alone far from our campsite. I speared a red deer. While I was skinning it, a lioness who wanted my kill jumped me, mauling my face. As she tore apart the deer, I was able to crawl under some bushes. Full with her meal, she left. I stayed there for days in a stupor of pain."

Anooka looked away from his face. "The men

of the clan must have come searching for you."

"I hid from them, letting them think me dead," he said.

"Why?" Anooka asked.

"I did not want anyone to see my disfigurement," he answered. "I lived through four seasons like a small animal, wary and cunning. I tried out mixtures of herbs, bark, fungus, and leaves for my wounds. My face slowly lost its rawness . . . the pain disappeared."

For the first time, Anooka looked directly at the claw marks on his face with admiration instead of discomfort—*he had healed himself.*

Durgun took another deep breath. "I made a singing bow to accompany the songs I created. I taught myself to carve. When I finally returned to the clan, it was as a man who has been tested by the Spirits."

"You came back as a shaman," Anooka said in awe.

He nodded, then moved his fingers restlessly over his robe until they stopped at the mended gash. "Your bearskin keeps me warm, Anooka, but this is the spot I love the best. You proved to yourself that you could make a correction after a mistaken act."

Anooka flushed. "Lacing up that cut was a small thing."

"Not so small. It made me know that you can change . . . like the river." Then Durgun spoke in an intense whisper. "I admire your spirit—find a way to use it well!"

He sank back, as if exhausted with pain and the effort of speaking.

Although she dreaded seeing her father, Anooka hoped he would return soon with the willow leaves. She smoothed back the damp hair from Durgun's face and pulled the robe up to his neck.

He glanced at the bow above him, then at her. She brought down the instrument and put it into his hands. He was too weak to play, but she was certain he would hear in his mind the low, haunting music.

CHAPTER TWELVE:
THE VIGIL

Sitting beside Durgun, Anooka heard only the sounds of his harsh breathing and the crackling of the little fire. When wolves began to call to each other in the night, she rose to close the flap. The howling continued and Anooka shook her head over her useless gesture.

Time moved slowly. She added wood to the fire. She filled Durgun's wooden cup with water and checked to see that there were round stones heating in the fire.

Anooka wished her mother were with her—she would be sure to have some potion to cure Durgun, some way to repay his gift to her of healing skills. But RavenWoman was walking to the west . . . of no help to the gift-giver.

Anooka remained by Durgun's side far into the night. Only once did he open his eyes. He looked at her and tried to shape his mouth into a smile of reassurance. Touched by his effort, Anooka smiled back—but she was not reassured.

She started when she heard quick, light steps outside. Her father entered the hut.

Tor's eyebrows went up when he saw her, but he nodded without speaking. Wearily dropping one shoulder, he let his pouch slide down to the ground. He bent over the shaman.

Anooka waited to hear that Durgun would be all right. There was only silence. "He hasn't spoken since nightfall, Father, although he smiled at me."

Tor pointed to his pouch. "Heat water for the willow tea. He must drink all he can."

Glad to be of use, Anooka took the leaves from the pouch, broke them into small pieces, and put them into Durgun's cup. With a horn spoon she scooped up round, hot stones from the hearth and dropped them into the water.

While the leaves were steeping, Anooka squatted in the back of the hut and gazed at her father. His face was a mask, but his sagging body told her more. Durgun was very ill.

When the leaves had brewed, Anooka removed the stones from the tea. After Tor raised up Durgun, she held the drink to the shaman's lips.

Durgun weakly grasped her shoulders and drank it down, sighing as he was lowered back to the bearskin.

"The clan has to know about Durgun," Tor said. "You and Nomi must tell them."

Angry tears sprang to her eyes. "Don't send me away."

"Go."

He did not look at her as she left.

In the family hut Nomi looked up sharply when Anooka entered. "Where have you been?"

"Durgun is ill," Anooka said dully. "We need to tell the others."

With a short cry Nomi grabbed her parka and was ready to leave.

They stopped at all the huts at the edge of the clearing. After they had told their news, the clanpeople flowed out of their huts to be with one another and talk.

"Sick? How long has he been sick?"

"Without him the salmon will stop running."

"Who will heal our healer?"

The sisters returned to their hut and slipped under their night-robes. In the dark, Anooka turned to Nomi. "Father was strange tonight—hardly speaking, demanding to be alone. Have you ever seen him like this before?"

"After Chee's death," Nomi said quietly.

Anooka shivered. She fumbled for the pendant and held it while she waited for sleep. When it came, she dreamed of a thin salmon-skin cape that floated in the sky before coming down to touch the high flames of a bonfire. As it burned, its color changed from gray to orange to lavender. Then the brilliant cape rose undamaged from the fire, swirling and soaring in the air before disappearing.

The next day, as Nomi slept, Anooka quietly left as the sun began its rise. She hurried to the pine forest. A handful of somber people waited outside the shaman's hut.

Owl frowned at Anooka. "No one can enter."

Without a word Anooka went inside. The hut was gloomy, the fire almost out. Her father was trying to raise Durgun to a sitting position, but the shaman's body was limp.

Tor lowered him back to the bearskin and spoke in a voice filled with resignation. "He spoke to me only once during the night. It took such effort . . ." Then his tone regained its authority. "There is no need for you here."

"I won't go!" Anooka said.

Her father folded his arms. It was the wrong time to argue with him—and useless.

Anooka left the hut with a knot in her stomach. She avoided looking at Owl, certain that the old lady's expression would be one of victory.

CHAPTER THIRTEEN:
TRANSFORMATIONS

Longing to be alone, Anooka walked slowly to her cave. Her clay animals sat side by side on the bark shelf. Were they forbidden to her? With one finger she caressed the wolf cub, the piece she had chosen to take to Durgun.

She sat before her hearth staring at the cold ashes. It seemed such a long time ago that she had warmed herself before the flames.

Anooka's eye was caught by a small, reddish piece in the ashes. She picked it up. This must be the fragment that her father had angrily thrown into the fire. A transformation had taken place! It was hard as stone.

Anooka sat still, the clay in her hand, her breath in her throat. Could this have happened to the bear she had thrown into the fire when arguing with her father? She put the fragment on the bark shelf and ran back to the family hut.

Nomi was gone. Thick layers of bone, ash, and charcoal filled the hearth. Anooka knelt and thrust her fingers deep into the muck, digging and sifting. Finally she held in her hand three small pieces of the shattered bear. They felt like rocks!

Anooka's mind raced. *Twice my clay has hardened—both times the change came through fire.*

She jammed the pieces of the clay bear into her shoulder pouch and started back to Durgun's hut. She must tell him what had happened. Only he would grasp its meaning and importance.

In the shadowy pine forest, a sense of foreboding swept over Anooka. Then she heard the sounds of sorrow—women weeping and one man's low, continuous cry. She knew that Durgun was dead.

She ran away from the mournful cries toward the river. When she was out of breath, she sank down on the bank. Burying her face in her hands, she sobbed without restraint.

When she finally pulled her hands away from her face, they were streaked with grime. The funeral would be tonight. Anooka took off her clothes and forced herself into the cold river to wash herself for the ceremony.

It was almost dark when she returned to the

family hut. Nomi was there, dressed in her finest clothing. Anooka glanced with dismay at her own charcoal-smudged tunic.

"I've been waiting for you," Nomi said.

Anooka's tears began again when Nomi gently touched her wet hair and swollen eyes.

"Wear one of my tunics," Nomi said. "And I have something else for you." She brought down a pair of boots from a concealed place in the roof. "I was going to give you these when I left in the fall. I give them to you now."

Anooka clasped the boots to her chest, then held them out to look at them. They were trimmed with braided strips of the same bleached leather that Nomi had used for her new pouch.

Anooka tearfully hugged her sister. "They're beautiful. I'll dress quickly—don't wait for me."

Nomi turned to leave the hut. "Hurry."

Anooka put on the tunic and new boots, then removed the pendant from its hiding place. Durgun had made this—she would wear it tonight to honor him. She took sinew from Nomi's sewing pouch and drew it through the little hole in the top of the pendant. She dropped the necklace over her head.

Anooka was one of the last to join the procession of clanpeople on their way to the pine forest. Owl, moving slowly, was near the back. The old woman scowled as her eyes darted from

Anooka's face to the pendant. Anooka raised her chin and kept walking.

A shallow burial pit had been dug near the shaman's hut. A high bonfire burned near the grave. Shivering without her parka, Anooka stood close to the flames. In the shifting firelight she looked for her father, but could not find him.

Nomi waited with the women on the other side of the bonfire. Anooka raised a hand to her in silent greeting. Nomi responded by putting a closed hand over her heart. Then she opened her fingers as if releasing a little bird who would fly to her sister to give her comfort.

Anooka nodded, her eyes filled with tears. She stood waiting for the funeral to begin. Without Durgun, how could the clan hold a ceremony? His hut looked small beneath the towering pines, but it held his body, his spirit. She heard the distant murmuring of the salmon-filled river, his river, and knew it would be running white in the moonlight. The shaman was still at the center of this ceremony.

The men began a low, repetitive chant for the dead. The voices of the women wove themselves into the song. Although she stood apart from them, Anooka tried to blend her voice with theirs. The sounds that came from her tight throat were toneless whispers.

Toward the close of the chant, three men left the group and entered Durgun's hut. Her father was with them when they came out. Each man held a corner of the bearskin robe with the shaman in the center. As the men pulled against one another to keep the robe tightly drawn, Anooka's fingers tightened as if she, too, were holding the bearskin taut.

Durgun, resting on his robe, was lowered into the shallow grave. Anooka made herself look at him. His face was tranquil, no longer tensed against his pain. He was dressed in a tunic richly beaded with small disks of ivory. Strands of salmon vertebrae hung around his neck, wrists, and ankles. His long, gray-streaked hair was spread out on the bearskin. Around his forehead was a carved ivory headband.

The four men returned to the hut. They came out holding the shaman's possessions and laid them near the grave.

Her father lifted the salmon-skin cape, then folded it and slipped it under Durgun's head. Anooka looked up, half expecting to see the brilliant cape of her dream soaring above her. Tor stroked the singing bow once, the last time it would be heard, then gently placed it on the shaman's chest. Anooka had a flash of resentment when her father handed the wooden tray that held Durgun's potions to Owl, although she knew that the old woman's age and experience made her best suited to use them well. The deerskin pouch that contained Durgun's flint carving tools was placed by the shaman's right hand. Then Tor held high the little ivory horse with the furry winter coat before laying it next to the flint tools.

Her father moved a short distance from the grave. He planted his legs slightly apart, a hunter's stance for strength and balance. Like one person, the clan leaned forward to listen:

"People of the Salmon Clan, our shaman has left us
To begin his great journey to the Spirit World.
People of the Salmon Clan, when he reaches his destination,
He will dwell with the Spirits and become even more powerful.
People of the Salmon Clan, when our shaman pleads for us,
The Spirits will be soothed by his songs and his singing bow.
People of the Salmon Clan, Durgun will always protect us,
And our river will run shining with salmon spring after spring."

Anooka had never heard her father speak like this. It was the firm, rhythmic voice that Durgun had used at ceremonies. She looked closely at the faces of the clanpeople. Their fears had been quieted.

At a gesture from Tor, people came up to the burial pit to make their contributions to the shaman. Owl was first with a finely stitched cap of ermine. Nomi gave the fawn-skin cape she had made as a gift for her future husband. A hunter left a roasted haunch of deer for Durgun's long journey. Children added berries and nuts. A young boy hesitated, then left his small bone harpoon behind.

After all the offerings had been made, Anooka opened her pouch and walked to the graveside. She placed the fire-hardened head of her clay bear in Durgun's hand and closed his fingers over it.

A praise-song to Durgun began. One by one people sang of his spiritual powers or his ability to heal; his thrilling dancing or his carving skills. The entire clan would then echo each of his attributes. Anooka sang steadily throughout the long chant, her throat loosened at last.

Tor gently rubbed fine red powder over Durgun's face to restore its glow of life. Then Anooka, with all the others, helped cover the burial pit with earth, then with water-smoothed stones.

When a low mound of stones had formed over the grave, Tor held his hands out in front of him, palms up, and nodded. The ceremony was over. The clanpeople drifted away, their muted conversations fading into the darkness. Nomi stopped to wait for her, but Anooka waved her on.

Finally only she and her father stood by the grave.

Anooka approached him nervously. "You comforted the clan, Father."

He looked at her, but made no answer. It was like him to say nothing, but she was stung by his silence. "You knew I wanted to stay with Durgun," Anooka said. "Why did you make me leave?"

"Because I wanted to be alone with him at the end." Then her father began to speak in such a low voice that she had to move closer to hear him. "I wasn't with Chee when he died . . . no one comforted him during his fear, his pain. . . ." He fell silent, his face more open and vulnerable than she had ever seen.

"You wanted a boy," she said.

He looked away. "I have things to teach a boy."

"And I know none of them," she said sharply. Too sharply.

"And why should you?" he demanded. "Don't criticize me for trying to raise you to be a clan-woman!" His eyes discovered the pendant. He grabbed it so forcefully that the sinew bit into the back of her neck. "Did that healer— RavenWoman—give you this?"

"No!" Anooka said. "I found it long ago buried in the floor of the hut."

Tor spread his fingers and let the pendant fall back onto her chest. "One more thing she left behind."

"What else did Mother leave?" Anooka asked.

"You, Nomi, and me," he said through clenched jaws.

Anooka felt a chill deep inside.

"Your sister told me that you received an invitation from this woman to meet her at the river fork at the next full moon," he went on. "And last night Durgun struggled to tell me you had discussed it with him." His tone was challenging. "When was I going to hear of this?"

"Mother made me promise not to speak to anyone who could prevent me from joining her," Anooka said.

"She meant me, of course." His chest heaved with labored breathing. "Anooka, you have rejected the ways of our clan. You have made it very clear that you want another kind of life."

She tried to keep her voice calm. "I do."

He locked his eyes with hers. "Then you are free to seek it."

Surprise silenced her for a moment. "Does this mean I have your permission to go to Mother?"

"It means you don't need my permission," he said. "Do what you will!"

CHAPTER FOURTEEN:
PREPARATIONS

They walked home in silence, their steps quick and hard on the path. Nomi was asleep when they returned to the dark hut.

Anooka took off Nomi's tunic and put her new boots aside. She burrowed under her bison robe, welcoming the warmth and familiar smell of the rough fur. She grasped the pendant tightly. Durgun had made it . . . Durgun who understood her and admired her spirit. But Durgun was dead.

She knew her father had given her the freedom to do as she wished out of anger, not compassion. Now she could live a life of her own choosing, but Anooka felt uneasy—less triumphant than abandoned. And Nomi would leave in the fall, just when Anooka thought they were becoming closer.

Now there is nothing to keep me here, nothing to keep me from going to Mother, she said to herself. She was startled by the wild, strange laughter of hyenas in the distance, and the calls made her worry about the lonely journey ahead. She would have to protect herself, get enough to eat, sleep without the security and comfort of the hut, and find her way to the river fork. And would her mother be there waiting for her? She turned restlessly in her bedding, finally drifting into a troubled sleep.

The sound of a soft wind blowing woke her. Anooka opened her eyes to see her father blowing the coals in the hearth to life.

Nomi sat on her night-robe braiding her hair. Her eyes narrowed when she saw the necklace around Anooka's neck. "Where did you get that?"

"I found it long ago," Anooka said. "Mother must have left it behind."

"Another secret," Nomi said angrily. "What right do you have to wear it? She was my mother, too."

Anooka pulled the necklace over her thick hair and held it out to her sister. "Take it."

Nomi made a sharp gesture of refusal. "It's no more mine than yours."

Anooka yanked open her shoulder pouch and dropped in the necklace. "I'll return it to its owner."

Nomi's eyes were wide. "Then you're going?"

"Yes!" There, it was said.

With his back to Anooka, Tor fed kindling to the fire. "You've complained that you don't have the skills to make such a journey."

Nomi broke in. "Father, you can't let her go!" She looked at Anooka with alarm. "You could be killed!"

"Mother lived," Anooka said.

Sitting on his heels, her father faced her. "The moon is rounding . . . time is short."

Anooka got up. Quickly she put on her soot-streaked tunic, her trousers, her old boots. She stuffed her fur hat and leather mittens into her shoulder pouch. She snatched her skin parka down from its hook, rolled it into a ball, and tried to cram it in.

"That pouch is too small to hold what you'll need. And your fur bedding is too heavy to carry," Tor said. He pushed open the flap and was gone.

She knew that everyone would soon find out that she was leaving the clan. Perhaps this was better than disappearing in the dark—like her mother. She tried to push away her confused feelings of disloyalty, hurt, and anger.

Anooka looked her sister's tight face. "Nomi . . ."

"You've made up your mind," Nomi said coolly.

Anooka was quiet for a moment. "The new boots you gave me are wonderful. I'll save them for best."

Nomi gestured toward the shoulder pouch, her harsh expression fading. "Is that all you're taking?"

"It's all I have," Anooka said.

"No, there's more." Nomi handed Anooka the tunic that she had worn at the funeral ceremony. "And your little animals are dear to you. Take some with you."

"I can't—they'll break." Searching through her pouch, Anooka took out two reddish fragments of fired clay. "I'll take these."

"Why take rocks?" Nomi asked.

"They're broken pieces of the bear I threw into the fire," Anooka said. "I don't understand it, but they hardened in the flames. I put the third piece in Durgun's hand last night because I wanted him to know what had happened. I hope he'll show it to the Spirits."

"He will," Nomi said.

Owl hobbled into the hut. With an uncomfortable look on her face, she dropped on Anooka's bedding a well-used backpack and a worn sleepskin made of two thin hides laced together.

"Why are you giving me this?" Anooka asked.

"My traveling days are over. Tell Lulaq I'm glad she lives." Owl left abruptly.

Anooka stared at the unexpected gifts. For the first time, she felt gratitude toward the old woman.

Her father returned and offered Anooka three smoked pieces of salmon. This time she accepted the food.

"I must be able to light a fire," Anooka said.

Tor gestured to the firesticks that lay by the hearth. "Be sure to keep your fire burning through the night."

Visions of savage predators—and Durgun's clawed face—filled her mind. Anooka concentrated on repacking her gear and spoke when she felt her voice was steady. "I need a weapon. May I have the little spear that's stuck under the roof? It's been there for so long."

"Too long," he said softly, bringing down the ivory-tipped spear. He handed her the finely made weapon without looking at it.

Nomi had been watching the preparations closely. "You must have mending tools!" She thrust her sewing pouch into the backpack, then helped Anooka attach Owl's sleep-skin to the pack with strips of braided leather.

After Nomi attached the pack to her sister's shoulders, Anooka turned and hugged Nomi close.

"Follow the river all the way to the fork no matter how it winds or doubles back," Tor said.

Anooka nodded, not trusting her words or her ability to hold back her tears.

Her father held open the flap. "Hurry—your race with the full moon begins."

CHAPTER FIFTEEN:
NIGHT CREATURE

Anooka squared her shoulders and strode through the crowded clearing.

"The Salmon Spirit will protect you if you stay close to the river," a man said loudly.

"Travel safely, Anooka!" a woman's warm voice rang out.

Anooka heard an older man mutter under his breath, "Foolish child—her mother's daughter."

Looking straight ahead, Anooka headed for the riverbank. She felt the unfamiliar weight of the pack with every step. Her old boots offered neither the padding nor the warmth of the new, white-banded pair she had worn last night.

Even the short spear was heavy in her hand.

Owl's two grandsons were coming down the path toward her, each walking with a hunter's swagger. A limp fox was draped around one boy's neck. A dead rabbit hung by a leather thong from the other's belt. They were boasting about what their snares had trapped and barely noticed her.

When they were out of sight, Anooka walked on to the place where the ledge leading to her cave jutted out above her. She stopped. Nomi had urged her to take some of her animals with her. She would find room for one.

With the bulky pack on her back, Anooka strained to make the climb to the ledge. Once inside the cave, she quickly picked up the wolf pup from the shelf. *Durgun will never see you, but you and I will make the journey together*, Anooka said to herself. She wrapped the pup in the scrap of fur she had used to kneel upon and tucked it into her shoulder pouch.

Returning to the riverbank, Anooka walked without stopping along a path that grew increasingly indistinct. When it disappeared she knew she was leaving the territory of the Salmon Clan.

Walking more slowly without a path to follow, Anooka worried about her pace. To set a brisk rhythm for herself, she began to sing a lively hunting song:

"Bison horn, fur of fox;
Horse's hair, soft wool of ox.
Red deer meat, brown bear skins;
Lion's tooth—the hunt begins!"

Singing the song over and over helped her move rapidly through the morning. The sun was overhead when Anooka stopped for food and rest. She sat down heavily on a flat rock that hung out over the river and let the pack drop from her aching shoulders. She removed her boots and rubbed her painful feet.

Anooka got out a piece of salmon from her pack. Watercress was growing on the far side of the river. She removed her trousers and hiked her tunic up around her waist. She picked up a bare branch, waded into the river, and probed the bottom with her branch. Soon she was thigh deep in rushing water so cold it brought tears to her eyes. But she returned smiling to the rock with the watercress and ate the wet, pungent leaves with the dry salmon.

The sky began to cloud up. She put on her hat, mittens, and parka, but knew that the jacket was too thin to shield her from heavy rain or wind. Nomi had twice offered to help her make a fur-lined parka. How foolish she had been to refuse.

She had told Nomi that she would not wear her new boots while on the journey. Anooka stuffed her old boots with soft moss before putting them back on. She would keep her promise.

Anooka realized with a jolt that darkness—and danger—would come soon. She put down her pouch and backpack and raised her spear over her shoulder. She tried to copy the young boys who threw real or imaginary weapons at every target they could see or imagine. But after repeated throws at a nearby bush, her motions remained slow and awkward.

When the sun disappeared behind clouds, she gathered up her things and moved on. Brooding over her clumsiness with the spear, she didn't have the heart to sing the hunting song. In the heavy mist, rocks and trees lost their sharp outlines. Only the sounds of the river remained constant as she walked beside it.

Anooka failed to watch what was beneath her. Her boot caught on a tangled vine, and she went down hard, the air knocked out of her. Struggling to her feet, she paused to catch her breath. Some distance away two shapes floated in the mist toward the river—a doe and her fawn. Her father would have speared one of them.

As the doe spread her legs to drink at the water's edge, the fawn bent to drink its mother's milk. Anooka stood still, delighting in the fidgety watchfulness of the doe and the gawky movements of the fawn. Her fingers moved as she thought about how she could capture them in clay.

The deer held no danger for her, but what about other creatures that might come to the river to drink during the night? It was late—she must gather fuel to make her fire. When Anooka began to collect wood, the doe raised her head sharply, ears twitching and water streaming from her mouth. She looked straight at Anooka, then turned and bounded away. After a moment of confusion her fawn followed.

"I wouldn't have hurt you," Anooka called out after them.

She gathered dead branches and stacked the wood near a boulder that still held the warmth of the sun. Beside it Anooka spread Owl's bedding. She had never slept alone before or outside the protection of a hut.

Using grass to start her fire, she twirled one upright fire stick between her palms against the one she held flat on the ground with her foot. No tendrils of smoke appeared. Anooka removed a bit of moss from one of her boots and used it instead of the grass. She twirled the fire stick again and smoke curled up from the moss. She blew on the tinder, then carefully added kindling.

When the little fire blazed, Anooka took off her mittens and hat and held them close to the flames. How warm they felt when she put them on again. She was hungry but tired—she needed sleep more than food. She laid her knife and spear next to the bedding. The soft backpack would make a cushion for her head. Anooka slipped into the sleep-skin fully clothed but still felt the shock of the cold, stiff bedding. The overcast sky was black above her. She had never felt so alone. Her father had said to keep the fire burning through the night. *Did I gather enough wood?* Her eyes became heavy. *How can I be sure I'll wake up to keep the fire going?* The questions went unanswered as she fell into an exhausted sleep.

Anooka woke with a start. The night vibrated with repeated, pulsating roars—the bellowing of a male lion! The roars were like low, aching moans and seemed to come from every direction. They were so loud and deep that she felt the air around her move in waves of sound.

She pushed herself down in the bedding until it covered her head, then pressed her hands against her ears to escape the terrifying noise.

Is my fire still burning? Anooka made herself get up. The fire was almost out. She added wood to the sputtering flames. They blazed into renewed life.

But the roars continued. Anooka's heart

raced. Her mouth was so dry that her tongue stuck to the roof of it. She stood close to the fire, her back against the boulder. One hand clutched her knife. The other gripped her spear.

CHAPTER SIXTEEN:
CIRCLE OF FIRE

Anooka turned her head back and forth, back and forth, searching for glistening eyes. Nothing. Blackness.

The roars continued, splitting the night.

Slowly the intervals between them increased.

At last they stopped altogether.

An unnatural silence fell, broken only by the soothing sounds of the river. The noises of the night gradually returned. Anooka welcomed as never before the trill of crickets, the croak of frogs, the drawn-out wail of a distant wolf. *Wolf.* Anooka felt around in her shoulder pouch. After adding more wood to her fire, she held the clay pup to her chest and stroked the fur it was wrapped in. Sitting close to the warmth of the fire, she half crooned, half hummed a clan lullaby:

"Little one, precious one — sleep, now sleep
Like the cub in its cave,
the pup in its den,
the bear in its lair.
Little one, precious one — sleep, now sleep."

The night lightened when a brief break in the clouds revealed the moon. Anooka's heart skipped — it would reach its fullness soon.

She closed her eyes to shut out the moon, to calm her fears. Singing the lullaby as if it had no beginning or end, she soothed herself to sleep.

Anooka woke to a gloomy dawn. She was slumped against the boulder, the clay wolf still cradled in her arms. Her fire was low but still burning. She bowed her head in gratitude — the flames had kept her safe.

She got up stiffly and searched the area around her campsite for tracks or leavings. There were none. Her empty stomach gnawed and growled, but she had to move on. She threw dirt on the fire and picked up her gear. As she started walking downriver, her legs ached, her back hurt. She forced herself to sing the hunting song; her feet fell into its rhythm. But when she sang of the hunter's quest for a lion's tooth, the terror of the night returned.

Anooka stopped singing when she thought of a lion's large, well-padded paws. She must hear everything around her, hear danger before it was upon her. She must be as alert as the doe at the river. Anooka heard every rustle, hum, and murmur that she had ignored before.

Even before she felt rain on her face, she heard the soft ping of a dry leaf being struck by a droplet. She drew her hat over her forehead and pulled up the hood of her parka. The rain turned hard and steady. The ground grew muddy and sucked at her boots, but Anooka trudged on. She felt the wetness through her boots first, then through her parka and mittens.

Watching for slippery vines and rocks, Anooka walked on as fast as she could. She would skirt a shallow puddle just ahead.

She stopped, her body rigid. The puddle was a huge paw print filled with rainwater!

Anooka gulped in air. Her muscles tensed. She wanted to run to safety—but there was no safety. The lion would follow her regardless of the direction she took.

She hurried on. RavenWoman would be waiting at the fork—she would know what to do. The river swerved in a wide arc. She thought she could make faster time by going straight ahead, but she had promised her father to follow the river.

At the water's edge Anooka came upon two

blurred footprints. She bent to examine them. Human footprints! *They could be Mother's footprints.*

But what if they weren't? When had they been made? Had her campfire been seen? Was someone hiding from her, perhaps unfriendly?

Hunger made her break off a piece of smoked salmon in her pack. She ate it greedily as she hurried on. Anooka started to grab a handful of unripe blueberries that grew by the river, but stumbled on a broken spear shaft half concealed by the berry bush. The polished wood glistened with rain. The point of the spear was gone.

Someone had been here by the river. Or was still here! Someone whose weapon had been shattered. Was the lion the hunter or the hunted?

She wanted to flee to safety, to return to the clan. *But I have no clan,* she said to herself. Under a sky the color of stone, she walked on without stopping, turning her head constantly to look behind and to either side. The sounds she heard merged with those she imagined—animal and human footsteps.

The raw, rainy day began to darken into night. Anooka stopped walking only when the rain stopped falling. Her first thought was of fire and fuel. She hurried to find some wood dry enough to feed a fire. The light was almost gone when she discovered a heavily leafed tree that sheltered dry, dead branches under its dense canopy.

She reached up and hung on to a branch until her weight brought it down. One branch, then another and another. Her hands hurt, but her woodpile slowly grew. Darkness finally made her stop.

She looked around for a cave or a boulder to offer protection. There were neither. How could she stay out in the open, completely exposed, and hope to fend off the lion?

I will surround myself with fire! Anooka picked out a small area of flat ground and dragged her branches there. She built five small pyres in a circle, putting the rest of the wood in the center. She would keep her fires burning through the night—danger would make sleep impossible.

What could she use as tinder to get her fires started? The moss in her boots was soaked. Anooka came across a hard, wet ball of dung. Stamping on the ball, she found it dry inside. Stepping into the middle of her circle, she put a bit of dung on the fire stick on the ground. Anooka twirled the other fire stick in its notch. Wispy smoke curled up.

Carefully she fed dry leaves to the smoldering tinder, then transferred the little blaze to one of her pyres. She ignited the four others with a burning branch from the first.

Trying to keep down her fear, Anooka closed her eyes and breathed deeply. She opened them to find two yellow-green eyes staring at her from the darkness beyond the fires. After a long, frightening moment of absolute quiet came a menacing snarl.

Anooka grabbed her spear and knife, her heart throbbing in her chest.

The eyes came closer. The snarling lion began to prowl around the fire circle. He could easily leap inside, but his fear of fire was holding him back. *So far.* Never letting go of her spear, Anooka concentrated on keeping her fires burning.

Her senses were so alive that she could smell the odor of rot—as if this lion were deathly ill. He was waiting her out. Or waiting for her fires to go out.

Suddenly the lion swung away, his glistening eyes vanishing. But the growling, no longer so close, mounted in intensity.

Above the snarls, but with the same urgency, came a choked cry: "Anooka, help! I need a weapon!"

CHAPTER SEVENTEEN:
TRACKING

She clutched her spear in one hand. With the other she snatched a burning branch from one of the fires.

Anooka sprang out of her circle of fire to follow the voice of her father.

"Over here!" he shouted.

Anooka held her torch high, but the night swallowed up the feeble light. "Where?" she cried out. "Tell me where?"

"Meadow!" He yelled louder. "Come quickly!"

Stumbling over the rocks and dead branches that littered the riverbank, she moved toward her father's voice. Once clear of the river she made better time.

Low snarls came out of the darkness.

She flinched. The sounds filled Anooka with fear, but they would guide her to where she must go.

Anooka came closer. The snarls grew louder.

She held her torch high. She made out her father standing in the meadow, his backpack clasped in front of him for protection. The lion was beyond him in the darkness.

Anooka raced to her father's side holding her upright spear out in front of her. He dropped his pack and grabbed the weapon. Positioning it over his shoulder, Tor leaned forward and hurled the spear toward the creature snarling in the shadows.

Anooka heard the dull thud of the spear as it struck flesh. The growling continued for a moment, followed by strangled breathing. She let out her own breath when she heard the heavy body fall to the ground.

"Give me the torch!" her father's voice rang out. "I must get the spear—it's our only weapon." She handed him the burning branch. As he hurried ahead, Anooka ran to catch up with him.

"Stay back!" Tor ordered. "He may be only wounded."

Tor raised the torch up and walked into the blackness. When he bent down, lowering the light, Anooka saw the great, sprawled body of the lion.

"He's on his way to meet the Lion Spirit!" her

father called out triumphantly. He ran back to Anooka holding both her spear and a spear point bound to a broken-off shaft.

She stared at the shattered weapon. "The other half of the spear I found yesterday was yours!"

"I didn't know the lion carried my spear point in his shoulder until tonight," he said. "I circled ahead of you trying to bring him down, but he disappeared into the brush. I thought I'd missed, but I couldn't find my spear."

"You've met this lion twice," Anooka said. "You've speared him twice."

Tor handed her the bloodied ivory-pointed spear. "I've been tracking him."

Anooka stiffened. "And me."

He was silent, but Anooka saw a small smile on his lips.

Returning to the fire circle, they found two fires sputtering; three were out. They brought all the wood together to make one large blaze.

"Why did you follow me?" she asked, grateful and angry at the same time.

"I'm still your father," he said quietly. "I asked that you stay on the riverbank because I wanted to know your pathway. There are several short-cuts to get to the fork. Now you can use them."

"You're turning back?" Anooka asked, ashamed of the alarm in her voice.

"If you want, I'll walk with you to the fork," he said.

111

Anooka looked into the blackness and searched for yellow-green eyes. "I'm glad—there may be other lions."

"This lion was alone, deserted by his clan, who are following the red deer far from here," Tor said.

"Why was he left behind?" Anooka asked.

"He must have been defeated in a fight with a younger male who has taken his place," he answered.

Tor squatted to examine the worn sleep-skin that Anooka was spreading on the ground. "Owl must have kept this bedding to remind herself of her old wandering life. She sleeps under fur now, but once she was as tough as any man."

"It's hard for me to imagine Owl young," Anooka said. "Everyone followed the herds when you were a boy. Isn't it better to stay in one place as we do now?"

"It's different," Tor said. "I remember the dancing and storytelling that followed success-ful hunts—and the hardship when food was scarce. In the old days no one complained about hunger, weariness, or the cold. In this way the clan could keep going and not be bur-dened by spoken troubles." He looked into the flames. "I grew up thinking I would live a hunter's life."

Like me, Father wanted another kind of life when he was young, Anooka thought.

He sighed with contentment as he slid into his bedding.

"You like sleeping outside, don't you?" Anooka asked.

"Look up," he said. "Stars are better than a smoky hut."

Anooka wriggled into her sleep-skin, drawing her legs up and wrapping her arms around her knees against the chill.

Tor stretched out to add another branch to the fire. "Your idea of building the little fires in a circle was good."

In the dark she smiled at his praise. Anooka rolled on her back and looked at the sky. The moon was almost round—*would Mother be waiting?* But she was comforted by the stars that were like a vast, sheltering roof above her.

She heard her father turn and turn again to find a comfortable position. "Sleep now," he said. "The walk tomorrow will be long and hard."

CHAPTER EIGHTEEN:
COMING CLOSER

Her father's sleep-skin was empty when she awoke the next morning. She guessed he was with the lion in the meadow. Anooka made herself leave what little warmth her bedding offered and pushed her feet into her stiff, mud-caked boots. She walked to the meadow to find her father sitting on his heels staring at the mangy carcass. It was pitted with old scars and newer open wounds.

"This lion was dying long before the spears found him," he said. "He was too old and sick to run down prey."

"Then he was no longer dangerous," Anooka said.

Tor shook his head. "He was more dangerous.

Hunger was driving him—look at his ribs." He pointed to the tail. "That's what smells . . . almost rotted off."

"Even so, will you take a tooth as your mark of bringing him down?" Anooka said.

"I'll take both fangs, although one is cracked throughout its length." Tor separated the undamaged incisor from the jawbone by working it back and forth with his hand, then used his knife to gouge out the damaged tooth. He walked to the river and scoured the teeth clean before dropping them into his shoulder pouch.

"We must move away from here," he said. "Hyenas will find this lion soon—I'm surprised they haven't already. Then the hunters of the sky will fly down to take what's left."

They returned to their camp and quickly packed up. Tor moved ahead noiselessly, springing off his back foot as the front one stretched forward. It took all of Anooka's effort to stay even with him. But after a morning of strenuous walking, she had learned to mimic the steady rhythm of his long, extended stride.

Anooka grew hungry. She thought of what her father had told her about the clan's old wandering ways—and remained silent.

Her father scanned the landscape as if he were memorizing the contour of the river, the plants that grew along its banks, the very rocks strewn along their path. He pointed out trees marked by wolf urine or bear scratches, then to a bit of blood next to a fluff of rabbit fur where a kill had taken place.

Anooka thought of how little time she had left with him and finally spoke. "The way you walk reminds me of Durgun."

"Why?" he asked.

"When he carved or danced, it was with all his care and concentration."

"I'm glad to be compared to Durgun," he said.

"You were close to him, weren't you?" Anooka asked.

"I was." There was a long silence. "He gave me support and guidance after Lulaq left. It was a difficult time for you and Nomi . . . for me."

Anooka was surprised and moved by his answer. For the first time she thought about how hard her mother's leaving had been for her father. "You were left with two small children," she said. "I was just a baby."

"Nomi was a great help," he said.

"She was so young when Mother left—how much help could she have been?" Anooka asked.

"I'll tell you," he said firmly. "For days you searched everywhere for your mother . . . crying . . . calling for her. Nomi tried to cheer you with your favorite foods, the little games you loved. She understood what your baby words meant. . . . I didn't even know they were words.

She sang you to sleep every night"—he looked straight ahead—"just as your mother did."

Anooka's face grew warm as she listened. Dropping behind, she put a closed hand on her heart, then opened her palm as if to release a little bird. *Nomi, my love flies to you.*

They walked steadily until the river made a wide swing, then left the bank to take a shortcut through a meadow of green grasses. Swaying in a light breeze, the grasses opened to reveal small purple flowers growing close to the ground. Now she wondered if these plants were useful in curing an illness or healing a wound.

Without the river rushing beside them, Anooka was suddenly aware of rustling, birdlike sounds. Looking up for their source, she almost walked into her father. He put a finger to his lips and pointed to a flock of partridges on the ground, then to her spear.

When she made too much noise putting down her backpack and pouch, he frowned. He shook his head when it took her too long to get her weapon into throwing position.

Tor mouthed the word "Now!" as the stout-bodied birds rose from the ground with a soft whirring of wings.

Anooka aimed her spear into the center of the moving mass and threw. The partridges wheeled away in an arcing formation—but one lay still on the ground.

"You've stunned your bird," he said. "This is your chance to do what hunters do and kill your prey."

She grasped the partridge with both hands. Its warm body pulsed with a delicate heartbeat. Aware that her father was looking at her, Anooka shut her eyes and made herself twist the bird's neck until the beating stopped.

"Attach the bird to your backpack," Tor said. "This will be a small meal for us tonight, but a good one." He held out deer jerky and sedge root he'd taken from his own pack. "This will keep us going until then."

They moved at a fast gait, but ate slowly to make the food last longer. They walked without stopping until the sun dropped below the mountains.

"We've covered a lot of ground," Tor said. "We'll camp here for the night."

"Father, take care of your spear while there's still some light."

Without another word, Anooka gathered wood and built a fire. She found some brown-speckled mushrooms and parsley fern that she cut into small pieces. Anooka stripped the bird of feathers, then cleaned and stuffed it. Binding the partridge with sinew, she ran it through with a green branch and balanced the stick on rocks placed on opposite sides of the fire she had started.

When the bird was cooked, Anooka gave one

half to her father, then singed her fingers and burned her tongue cramming the food into her mouth. She paused only to spit out feathers missed in the plucking. "The best meal I've ever had."

"It was good," Tor said, throwing his last bone in the fire. "You've complained that I didn't teach you what boys must learn, yet I saw you force yourself to kill your bird."

"I never said I wanted to be a hunter." Anooka heard the defensive tone in her voice, but could not change. "I started out for the fork unprepared, without the skills to feed and defend myself."

"I never imagined you would need such skills," he said. "If Lulaq travels alone between the western clans, I know she has good weapons."

"I saw nothing but a knife at her waist," Anooka said.

Tor shook his head dismissively. "She must have more protection than that." He picked up his spear again and expertly bound his old spear point to the new shaft with heated pine pitch and a strip of sinew.

"You're good at what you do," Anooka said, "just as I wanted to become good at making my animals." She took out her wolf pup, unwrapped it, and put it in his hands. "Look at it, Father. I made it thinking of the little wolf you brought me when I was young."

His expression softened as he ran his fingers over the piece. "You wanted me to return it to its mother—it was a long walk back to the den." He handed back the pup. "This is well made, Anooka."

Expecting anger, she had received praise. Nodding her thanks, Anooka continued. "On Durgun's last night, he asked me to bring him one of my pieces, but he died before I could show him this. He was going to tell me if I could continue making my animals."

Tor said nothing for a moment. "One of the last things Durgun talked to me about was your work with the strange mud you found a use for. He felt sure your figures were made to honor the Animal Spirits—like his own carving and dancing." Tor's voice deepened. "You felt you had to leave to have a different kind of life. I wish I had made it possible for you to stay—and be different."

Anooka gazed at her father and felt a tightening around her heart. "I'm glad to be your daughter."

"I have something to give you, Anooka, because you are my daughter—my brave daughter." Opening his shoulder pouch, he took out a lion's tooth and handed it to her. A small hole had been bored through its jagged, blunt end.

"But . . . but it's the whole tooth," she stuttered with surprise. "I would be proud to take the damaged one. It was you who stalked and killed the lion."

"Without your courage, I would have been the one killed," he said.

Anooka threaded twisted fiber from her sister's sewing pouch through the little hole. Knotting the ends together, she dropped the necklace over her head. "Father, I will never take this off."

CHAPTER NINETEEN:
THE FORK IN THE RIVER

They walked without words through the morning. Anooka stayed close to her father's side, her steps matching his. The sun was at its height when they rounded a bend. Two rivers swerved apart where one had been before. Anooka strained to see her mother, but no one waited at the fork.

Then a faint *toc toc toc* could be heard. Her father halted abruptly.

"She's waiting," he said. "That's her summons."

"I see nothing," Anooka said. "What summons?"

"The calls came from behind that boulder," he said, pointing. "That was Lulaq's signal to you and Nomi when you were small. When you heard it, you returned to her no matter where you were or what you were doing."

Now she knew why she had plunged into that wild place on the river to go to her on the opposite bank!

"Will you take me to Mother?" Anooka said, surprised at her own question.

His eyes looked pained. "Why should I do this?"

"So you can ask her to come back to us," she whispered.

His shoulders sagged. "Too much time has gone by. We've chosen separate paths. We will follow them."

She knew that nothing she could say would change his mind.

Anooka held out her arms. "Father, it's hard to leave you."

He embraced her hard and close. "Go to this RavenWoman who claims you, Anooka." Tor fingered the lion's tooth at her neck and smiled at her, although his eyes were wet.

He turned and started back with a fast, pounding gait, not the silent stride that had become familiar to her. Anooka's hand stayed motionless in the air while her father grew small in the distance. Finally he disappeared at a bend in the river.

The *toc* call came again. Anooka took off her

clothes and boots and stuffed them in her backpack. Quickly she washed herself in the river and forced her fingers through her tangled hair. She put on her new clothes, but let the lion's tooth stay hidden beneath her tunic.

She moved forward. Shielding her eyes from the sun, Anooka made out her mother, who now stood beside the boulder moving one hand in short, stiff waves. Anooka waved back, then hurried to cover the ground between them.

Anooka finally stood before her mother, hoping to be gladly received, even embraced. She was not. Anooka spoke to break the awkward silence. "I'm glad we've come together, Mother." She said the last word with a slight emphasis to remind herself that this striking woman was indeed her mother.

"Welcome, Anooka," RavenWoman said. "I thank the Spirits for your safe journey."

It's Father who deserves your thanks, Anooka said to herself, unwilling to tell her mother that she had not come to her alone.

Comparing herself to the commanding figure who stood before her, Anooka felt unadorned and awkward. From her mother's shoulder hung the amber-studded grass pouch. The fringe at the bottom of her tunic had been cut to resemble feathers. As before, her braids were plaited with strips of white fur.

Anooka pointed to the bird with outstretched

wings that had been singed into the front panel of her mother's tunic. "Nomi burned a design like this on her new boots. She told me she learned how from watching you."

RavenWoman leaned forward. "Nomi can remember that? She was so young when I—" Her face tightened, then relaxed. "What was her design?"

"Two mated geese traveling the seasons together," Anooka replied.

Her mother looked away. "Ah, Nomi will be a good wife."

Anooka nodded. "You spoke of my safe journey," she said, "but the trip was hard, at times frightening. Weren't you afraid when you left the clan?"

"I was unprepared for what I faced, but I learned self-reliance from my wandering," RavenWoman said.

Anooka pointed to the knife at her mother's waist. "You carry no other weapons. How do you travel safely between the western clans?"

RavenWoman smiled slightly, then motioned Anooka to follow her to a small, well-ordered campsite set back from the river. Kindling was stacked on a large, flat rock. Next to the wood were strips of deer meat and a pile of chokeberries. Fur-lined bedding lay spread on the ground. Her reed pouch and wooden bow hung from the branch of a tree next to the backpack.

Her mother removed the bow and pouch from the branch and held them out in front of her. "This is how I protect myself."

"With a singing bow?" Anooka asked in disbelief.

"A *hunting* bow, not a singing bow," RavenWoman said. Shouldering the pouch and grasping the bow, she retraced her steps to the river without looking back.

Anooka put down her possessions and ran to catch up. "Where are you going?"

"To a waterfall just below the fork," she answered. "It's a favorite place for catching salmon."

After walking some distance, her mother stopped and pointed to a small waterfall. More bears than Anooka had ever seen before were fishing in the white, turbulent water beneath the cascade. A huge dark bear dominated the scene. No other bear came near as it sat on its haunches grabbing at the salmon that passed by in the river. Large females tried to fish from the shore while their cubs got in the way by growling and tugging at their mothers' catches. Bears not fully grown nervously took their fish behind the bushes to eat far from the larger bears.

Eagles beyond counting wheeled and soared overhead. Others sat on the banks or perched in trees close to the river. Some left the branches to hover over the water with powerful wing beats.

Screaming at each other, they swooped down to tear at half-eaten salmon that the bears had abandoned in their gluttony.

Her mother pointed at a lone young wolf crouched motionless at the river's edge. Suddenly its broad, gray head moved forward into the water. It stood up with a writhing salmon in its mouth.

In one smooth motion RavenWoman reached over her shoulder to remove a small spear from her pouch. She rested its point on her clenched hand in the middle of the bow. Planting her feet firmly, she brought the bow up vertically with her extended left arm. Her right arm was tightly flexed with her fingers grasping the sinew string and the little spear. With a graceful, sudden movement, she brought them both close to her head.

RavenWoman narrowed her eyes and drew back the string with such force that it touched her right cheekbone. The wooden bow bent until it formed a half circle. "Watch—this will go farther and faster than any spear."

She was taking aim at the wolf.

Anooka raised both hands in the air. A strangled cry came from her throat. "Don't kill it!"

The wolf dropped the fish and swung its head in Anooka's direction. With her mouth set in a straight line, RavenWoman released her grip on the taut sinew. *Whoosh.* The wolf collapsed on the

riverbank with the point embedded in its throat. Anooka put her hand on her own throat, astounded by the force and speed of her mother's magical weapon. "I thought the little spear was a toy when you took it out."

"Not a toy—it's an arrow," RavenWoman said. "I'm a woman without great strength or height, but I am able to hunt and protect myself with this weapon." She turned to leave the river. "That wolf pelt is valuable, but it's too dangerous to go among the bears to skin it."

"You killed the wolf only to show me how deadly your weapon is!" Anooka said.

RavenWoman looked at her and nodded. Grasping the bow firmly, she set out for camp with a proud walk and a straight back.

On returning, Anooka looked at her ivory-tipped spear and compared it to the power of the bow and arrow. Her mother's eyes followed her gaze.

"That was your father's spear—when he was a boy," RavenWoman said in an unsteady voice. "He was saving it . . ." She broke off and busied herself with starting a fire.

For Chee, Anooka said to herself. Feeling tears gather behind her eyes, she turned away to spread her sleep-skin next to her mother's elegant bedding.

RavenWoman glanced down. "Your sleep-skin is old and worn."

"It was Owl's . . . from her wandering days," Anooka said. "She gave me her backpack, too."

"Owl!" RavenWoman said. "No one judged me more harshly."

"I have a message from her," Anooka said quickly. "She wants you to know she's glad you live."

Her mother's mouth opened in surprise; then her hand quickly covered her lips.

Again Anooka spoke to fill the silence. "How long will we stay here?"

"Only tonight," RavenWoman said. "Tomorrow we'll start for the nearest of the western clans. We'll stay there while you begin to learn the tasks you will perform in your new life."

"What will I need to know?" Anooka asked.

"It will take you a long time to learn which flowers, leaves, and fungi to gather to make my potions and salves." RavenWoman's words were precise. "I will teach you how to heat stones properly to lay over the tender places of those in pain. While I dance and chant at my healing ceremonies, you will learn how to blow smoke through a hollow bone over the bodies of those who seek my help."

"Won't they be seeking my help, too?" Anooka asked.

Her mother's head went back almost imperceptibly. Ignoring the question, she walked to the fire and deftly pushed the burning wood to one side with her knife. When she dropped the strips of deer meat on the hot stone, they sizzled as they seared.

RavenWoman resumed speaking. "You will also be responsible for keeping me supplied with a powerful medicine that has brought me fame."

Something about the way her mother looked at her made Anooka anxious. "What is this medicine?"

"You must keep my secret," RavenWoman said. "I cool fevers and heal burns with the fresh gallbladder of bears."

Anooka could not control a shudder. "Am I to kill bears to get it?"

"Only young bears—they're less dangerous," RavenWoman said. "After you learn to use a bow and arrow, you won't find it difficult."

"It would be difficult for me," Anooka said.

"I'm not surprised," her mother said. "Why did you try to stop me from killing the wolf?"

"I'm . . . I'm not sure," Anooka stammered. "It was so beautiful . . . young . . . it wasn't going to hurt us. . . ."

"You are tenderhearted," RavenWoman said. "There is little room for this in the life I offer you."

Anooka stared hard at her mother. "Durgun was kind and he was a healer."

RavenWoman's eyebrows shot up. "What do you mean—*was* a healer?"

131

"Durgun is dead," Anooka said softly.

Her mother closed her eyes as if to shut out the news.

"Just before he died, he told me how close he felt to you," Anooka said. "He thought he'd failed you when you left the clan."

"Durgun didn't fail me," RavenWoman said in a voice that seemed to lose itself in the dusky evening. "He listened and spoke with his heart."

Full of feeling, Anooka nodded in agreement. "Durgun told me that after the Spirits transformed him, he returned to the clan as shaman. You, too, have changed from the person you used to be. The Salmon Clan is without a—"

"I could not take Durgun's place," RavenWoman broke in and spoke in a passionate voice. "Durgun was transformed by the Spirits—I transformed myself!"

Anooka was awed by the force of her mother's answer. But through the day she had seen this strength disappear like a spring creek that goes underground only to reappear in another place—just as strong.

CHAPTER TWENTY:
ANOOKA'S ANSWER

In the late afternoon Anooka and her mother sat on their bedding opposite each other, eating the seared deer meat and sweet chokeberries.

The food was good, but Anooka could hardly swallow it.

She searched in her shoulder pouch and brought out her wolf pup. Removing its fur wrapping, she held it out on her palm. "You asked me why I didn't want the wolf killed. I found a special kind of mud that I use to make animals like this pup. I try to catch their essence, their energy. I don't want to kill them."

Her mother looked at the wolf without reaching for it. "You are clever with your hands, but there will be no time for this."

Anooka drew back the pup, startled by her mother's words. She could almost feel the moist, slippery clay on her fingers and thought of the animals she longed to make—an eagle with an open beak and a sleek young wolf with a salmon in its mouth. She would not show her mother the fragment that had turned into rock.

"Why can't I make my animals *and* learn what I must know?" Anooka said.

Her mother stared at her, finally saying, "You must perform your duties well in the important life I offer you."

"Important!" Anooka cried out, surprised at her own sudden fury. "What's important to you? Weren't the two children you left behind important?" She trembled as she spoke.

Her mother blinked several times. "Leave the past behind, Anooka." Then she bit her lip and turned away. "You're shivering—we'll be warmer in our sleep-skins."

Anooka watched her as she silently built up the fire and then prepared herself for sleep. Underneath her tunic was a close-fitting garment of soft squirrel skin. Underneath her boots were fur mittens for the feet that Anooka had never seen before.

When her mother unwound the braids that circled her head and began to remove the bands of white fur woven into them, Anooka sucked in her breath. The fur had been so cleverly plaited

that she hadn't realized her mother's hair was streaked with white.

RavenWoman looked at Anooka with a steady, calculating gaze. "I want you to see me as I am — no longer young."

Anooka's response was quick. "You want me to know that the day is coming when you will need someone to care for you."

Her mother flinched, but said nothing.

Anooka forced out words through a tight throat. "You don't want to remember that you were supposed to have taken care of me when I needed you."

"I told you that the past is past," RavenWoman said sharply.

Anooka did not trust herself to speak again. Silently she took off her new tunic and started to put on her old one for the night.

Her mother pointed to Anooka's necklace. "Tell me about the lion's tooth you've kept hidden," she said in a challenging tone.

Startled, Anooka covered the tooth with her hand — she had forgotten it was there. *Too many secrets,* Durgun had said. She dropped her hand. "I didn't know that Father had followed me on my journey to you until a lion came into my camp. He gave me this tooth after I helped him make the kill. Today we walked together to the fork." She paused. "He turned back when he heard your *toc* call."

"You broke your vow to me," RavenWoman said. "If he followed you here, he must have known of your decision to join me."

"There was no need to keep our plan hidden from him," Anooka said. "He had given me permission to live my own life."

RavenWoman spoke after a long silence. "Tor has been a good father to you and Nomi."

Anooka was aware of her own breathing. "I'm surprised to hear you say that."

"I could not have left if I had thought otherwise," RavenWoman said in a voice barely audible.

In the fading light, Anooka searched her mother's somber face and saw thin webs of lines at the outer corners of her eyes and mouth. "Mother, come home. You grow old without your people, without a clan . . ."

Her mother shook her head. "I think you want me to return as that long-ago woman, Lulaq."

"Who sang on the riverbank," Anooka murmured.

"I am RavenWoman now—I sing healing chants and nothing more." Her back straightened as she transformed herself again. "I need no one and no one stands in judgment over me. I *made* this life. I know what it demands and what it gives to me."

Anooka took in the force of her mother's words at the same moment she sensed the loneliness beneath them. "I admire the way you shaped the life you are living—and now I must shape my own," she said in a calm, clear voice. "I will continue to make my clay animals that I tried to keep hidden, but I will no longer work in secret." Anooka spoke without anger. "In the morning I will start my return to the clan."

RavenWoman's posture remained defiant, but her eyes looked away.

"Mother, I admire your strength, your courage," Anooka said. "I will need some of your spirit to create this new life for myself."

"Your spirit is strong, daughter . . . too strong to live well with mine," RavenWoman said. "And you have something as important that I gave up—a tender heart."

Anooka remembered what her mother had forgotten. She rummaged through her shoulder pouch until her fingers closed on the ivory pendant. "I have treasured this, but it belongs to you." She leaned across the bedding. "Durgun told me that the outer circles stood for the blossoming of your three children. Now they will be with their mother."

"I have yearned for this," RavenWoman said, reaching out to grasp the necklace. "I wish I could claim praise for your blossoming, 'Nooka. I cannot."

Anooka slid into her sleep-skin and watched the flames dance in the darkness as a wind came up. Its low moan made her remember her dream about the lion cub. *The cub should be done with whining and waiting,* she said to herself.

She lay on her back and looked up at the full, luminous moon and the sheltering stars. Anooka fumbled until she found and held her mother's hand.

CHAPTER TWENTY-ONE:
AWAKENING

The hooting of an owl broke through Anooka's sleep. The sky was brightening; the dawn had come. She nestled deep in her bedding listening to the haunting cries.

Finally she spoke to her mother. "The song of the owl reminds me of Durgun's singing bow."

There was no response.

Anooka sat up with a jolt.

Her mother was gone! Her sleep-skin was gone!

Anooka looked at the rock that had held the fire. Only ashes, but a pile of nuts and roots had been gathered there.

She leaped up and ran toward the riverbank.

"Mother!" Anooka shouted through cupped hands. "Mother! Mother!"

There was no answer.

She's disappeared — again. Without a word — again.

Anooka ran barefoot to the branch that had held her mother's belongings. The backpack was no longer there, but the grass pouch swung in the light breeze, its amber beads glittering like dew in the slanted morning sunlight.

Anooka snatched the pouch from the branch and held it against her cheek. Then she threw it down — hard. She wanted more than the pouch. *But my mother is RavenWoman now,* Anooka thought. *She would not have held me, she would not have wept as we said good-bye.*

Slowly Anooka picked up the pouch. Gently she shook off the dirt and leaves that clung to its fine weave and opened it. Inside was the black reflecting rock that the great northern hunter had given to his healer. Removing its wrapping, she peered at herself and saw hurt and disappointment in her eyes. Anooka walked to the river to bathe her face.

The icy water shocked her into action. She must move quickly to take advantage of the mild weather to start her journey home. Back at the campsite she packed her good tunic and boots. She would return the sewing pouch to Nomi with the obsidian mirror inside. Anooka carefully placed the delicate grass pouch in her backpack. She would keep it as her own.

She put the nuts and roots in her shoulder pouch to eat slowly as she walked. They wouldn't last long, but her mother had been generous to leave them for her. She would have to search for food as soon as she could.

Anooka stuffed her old boots with grass and thought of her mother's warm, protecting foot mittens. When she got home, she would ask her father for a bone needle and flint awl and make a pair for herself—and a pair for Nomi. She knew she had much to learn from her sister. After Nomi left the clan, perhaps she could learn from Owl. As they worked together, she would ask her about the old wandering days and listen to her stories.

She rolled up her sleep-skin and attached it to her pack. After fastening her knife to her belt, she shouldered her load. When she bent to pick up her spear, Anooka gasped. The hunting bow and pouch full of arrows lay half concealed behind a rock! Now her mother was as defenseless as she'd been when she left the clan so long ago. Anooka's heart swelled with gratitude.

Anooka started off with a rapid gait, thankful that the river would lead her home. To distract her mind from the weight of the pack and the long journey ahead, she concentrated on the water rushing beside her. Sunlight flickered like flames over its turbulent surface. Her body, sweaty from the fast pace she was maintaining, was sprayed by wind-driven mist, which cooled her and gave her new energy. Another gift—this time from the river.

In the early afternoon Anooka heard rustling nearby. Two rabbits darted from the bushes. She reached for the hunting bow and arrow pouch. It was an empty gesture—she had to learn how to use this new weapon.

She put down her load and notched one of her arrows in the bow's sinew string. Choosing a soft, rotting tree trunk as a target, she pulled back the sinew as she'd seen her mother do. But unlike her mother's fluid motions, her own were slow and unsure. When she released her fingers, her arrow dipped and slid on the ground before coming to rest far from the trunk.

Before the next shot, she thought of all the things her torso, arms, and fingers must do. So many things. She was tense with doubt. Her next arrow landed closer to the tree, but it had no strength behind it. Anooka was close to tears. In her hands the weapon had lost its magic.

Then she remembered her father just before he spoke at Durgun's funeral. He had planted his legs slightly apart—a hunter's stance. And her mother's feet had seemed to grip the ground

just before she released the arrow that killed the wolf.

Anooka removed a third arrow from the quiver. She deliberately positioned her legs for strength and balance. Shutting out everything but the feel of the riverbank beneath her feet, she squinted at the target and took careful aim before opening her fingers. At its release, the arrow sprang from the bent bow like a living thing and buried its tip in the soft tree trunk. She stared triumphantly at her target, then rapidly shot off the seven remaining arrows. Three missed their mark, but her body automatically made slight adjustments that corrected the error on the next shot.

While she collected the spent arrows, Anooka imagined her father's astonishment on seeing her demonstrate the weapon. She could see his smile as she thrust the hunting bow and quiver in his hands. It would be a gift for her father— from her mother.

Anooka also imagined the reaction of the clanpeople on her return. Now she knew her father would welcome her, as would Nomi and most others. Even Owl, she hoped. A few would taunt her. *Let them.* Anooka heard in her mind the sound of her scraper as it sliced through the bearskin. Hadn't Durgun told her that she'd proved she could make a correction after a mistaken move?

Twigs and gravel crunched beneath her boots as she retraced her steps along the river. As she moved through her journey, Anooka tried to see the landscape with her father's steady concentration. She watched for the silvery slide of salmon in the river; she was successful at spearing two that had come near the surface to spawn. She found and collected berries, grassy herbs and watercress, mushrooms, and roots almost without searching. The food she prepared for herself was good and ample.

Looking up from grilling a frog over a little fire, Anooka saw eagles circling in a tight formation over a spot near the bank ahead. She ate quickly, then took a wide detour away from the river. Let the hunters of the sky compete with the wolves and hyenas in picking a carcass clean.

At the end of each day Anooka gathered enough kindling at to keep her fire burning until dawn. To her surprise some part of her mind signaled her to get up and feed the flames throughout the night. Quickly returning to her sleep-skin, which now warmed her more than before, she felt sheltered by the starry roof above her.

After days of hard traveling, Anooka saw smoke in the distance and knew it was the fire in the clearing of the Salmon Clan. "Home," Anooka said out loud, liking the word and drawing out its sound. Hardly aware of the weight of her burdens, Anooka walked toward the clearing with the noiseless, gliding gait of her father, but with her shoulders back, like her mother.

AUTHOR'S NOTE

During the time and place of Anooka's story, 12,000 years ago in western Europe, the great herds of bison, horse, and mammoth that once roamed the continent were dwindling. Atlantic salmon, swimming by the millions to spawn in the rivers of their birthplace, became increasingly important as an alternative food source. Long before Anooka was born, her clan had given up the nomadic life of hunting and gathering to live by a fish-laden river. To make this new way of living succeed, a clan had to be large enough to gather, preserve, and store adequate numbers of salmon for the long winter months. Some prehistoric archaeologists believe that the first permanent settlements were based on cooperative fishing, not farming.

The idea for the spiritual significance of salmon comes from several sources. Historic records tell us that the almost vanished culture of the Ainus of northern Japan was dependent on salmon, the "divine fish" sent to the Ainus by the spirits. Until fairly recently, the Pacific Northwest Coast Native Americans also geared their survival to the arrival of spawning salmon to their rivers. Elaborate rituals of welcome were held to greet the first spring run.

Harpoons, important to Anooka's clan, were invented at least thirteen thousand years ago. These barbed tips of bone and antler were designed to pierce flesh and remain in place. They were produced in a variety of designs and sizes for a wide range of hunting and fishing needs. Ancient harpoons can be seen today in museums exhibiting prehistoric artifacts.

The bow and arrow was a brilliant invention based on the knowledge that sapling wood bends under tension and springs back when released. Using this new weapon instead of a spear, a hunter had greater range and power, the possibility of concealment and surprise, and the ability to shoot repeatedly at a target. The earliest intact bow and arrow found is 8,000 years old, but most prehistorians believe the weapon is much older. Small flint points resembling arrowheads have been dated at 17,000 years old, but wooden bows and sinew cords decay through time, making precise dating of the compound weapon impossible.

On the wall of a cave called Les Tres Frères in southern France, there is a powerful drawing of a dancing shaman-like figure surrounded by animals. He holds what many believe to be a bow-shaped musical instrument; it is the inspiration for Durgun's singing bow. Which came first, the musical instrument or the bow and arrow? And did the invention of one lead to the other? As with many questions buried in the prehistoric past, we will probably never discover the answer.

Knowledge of plants used for healing in the Upper Paleolithic is largely lost to us, but it is known that willow leaves and bark relieve pain because they contain a key ingredient of aspirin. From seventh-century Chinese records we know that bears were killed for the medicinal properties of their gallbladders; this practice is thought to be far older. Western medical science has now proven its value in healing. In spite of the availability of a synthesized drug, many Asians today pay high prices for the gallbladders of bears.

Anooka's discovery of the possibilities of clay modeling and simple hearth firing is based on the elusive archaeological record. Thousands of small *fired* clay animal and human figurines were recovered from a 26,000-year-old site in eastern Europe. The technology seems to have disappeared for ten thousand years, then reappeared in the Upper Paleolithic record with a fired clay bead and unfired clay animal sculptures. Although the evidence is sparse, it is plausible to speculate that Anooka could have brought to her own clan the art of working in clay. Utilitarian clay objects made for everyday use, such as hollow storage containers and drinking vessels, emerge in Europe two thousand years after Anooka's time.

Without the unity and stability of a clan, individual survival would have been almost impossible during the period in which this book is set. What helps hold a group together, then and now, is a shared belief system and established codes of conduct. The conflicts between traditional behavior and new ways of thinking must be as old as the human race.

Prehistoric archaeologists believe that neighboring clans formed social networks in order to arrange marriages, deal with conflicts, and engage in trade. Amber and seashells, for example, were widely traded; we know they were used decoratively because many were perforated. In the book, these mutual needs and dependencies are met by an annual meeting of nearby clans called the Gathering.

Although the setting and the life lived by Anooka and her people were vastly different from ours, we all share the same human capacity to feel hurt and anger, fulfillment and joy. What binds us together across thousands of years are these qualities that make us human.